All at once the feeling was there again. The magical feeling. The girl in the mirror smiled a slow, confident, meltingly beautiful smile. Something about this room released her—my secret, other self. Not the self whose clothes weren't right. Whose tongue turned to wood whenever there was a good-looking guy around. No. If the girl in the mirror went to a party, heads would turn and voices would buzz: "Who is that?" The guys would crowd around. She would laugh and know exactly what to say.

A soft yellow glow, like sunrise, spread over the mirror. Behind my right shoulder I saw reflected a hand, disembodied, hanging in the air. I twisted around, and it was still there, just beyond the window. It hovered for an endless moment, then one finger separated itself out from the rest and began to trace something in the dirt on the glass.

Available from Crosswinds

Dropout Blues
by Arlene Erlbach

Even Pretty Girls Cry at Night
by Merrill Joan Gerber

Angel in the Snow
by Glen Ebisch

the Haunting Possibility

SUSAN FLETCHER

CROSSWINDS

New York • Toronto
Sydney • Auckland
Manila

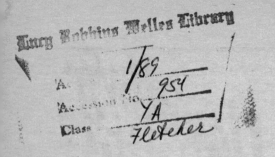
First publication March 1988

ISBN 0-373-98019-1

SUSAN FLETCHER graduated Phi Beta Kappa, with highest honors, from the University of California at Santa Barbara, and received an M.A. in English from the University of Michigan. She has worked as an advertising copywriter and radio producer and has written numerous articles for magazines including *Ms.*, *Mademoiselle* and *Woman's Day*.

Ms. Fletcher, her husband, her daughter and a black cat live in Lake Oswego, Oregon. *The Haunting Possibility* is her first novel.

Chapter One

The thought of moving into a haunted house never fazed me. It probably should have. I was agnostic on ghosts at the time, which is a dignified way of saying I couldn't make up my mind. The way I saw it, nobody's ever scientifically proved ghosts exist, but then nobody's ever proved they don't exist, either. They're a possibility. Anyway, ghosts were the least of my problems just then. I had much scarier things to think about.

It wasn't just moving to Oregon, thousands of miles from the friends I'd known all my life. Although that one had me feeling pretty low. No, what really petrified me was having to make friends in a town full of rich kids, while living in this hulking wreck of a house. And when Dad promised to have it shipshape in no time—*that* just about curdled my blood.

"Would you look at the potential in this house, Katie!" Dad actually turned around in the car seat as he pulled into the driveway, to make sure I fully appreciated all that potential. I was looking, all right. But all I saw was an ancient, stone-faced monstrosity with a steep roof which dripped moss and sprouted ferns. An insidious, gray-green slime crawled up the stones from the sodden ground. The Slime That Ate Oregon, I thought. The wooden window frames had a terminal case of rot, and where the panes didn't gape jaggedly, they were scarred with black mold spots. Like some prehistoric, tooth-gnashing monster—with zits.

"I've never seen such potential!" Dad threw open the car door and squished happily through the damp leaves that coated the front yard. Amy, my four-year-old sister, trampled me on her way over the seat and out Dad's door. Close behind, our pug dog, Cyrano, snorted across my lap.

"He'd see potential in a garbage dump," I grumbled.

"Hush," said Mom.

But it was true. Dad sees potential in everything. Which is probably why his "how-to-do-it" books sell so well. I mean, they aren't bestsellers or anything, or we'd be rich, which we definitely aren't. But Dad somehow makes you see beyond the crummy way things are to this wonderful vision of how they could be. The people who read his books eat it up. It sustains them while they're tightening lug nuts or linoleuming bathrooms or whatever.

Meanwhile, the Great Visionary was in hog heaven, stomping around in the drizzle and the muck. He exuded supreme confidence. "Yep. I'll have this baby shipshape in no time."

Here's where the old blood began to curdle. "Like you got the automatic sprinklers shipshape by flooding the neighbors for five days straight?" I muttered, too softly for Dad to hear.

"Hush!" Mom said.

"I thought old man Martin was going to build an ark."

"Kate! Exercise some restraint! Don't spoil it for him."

The thing is, whenever Dad promises to make something shipshape in no time, it's like the curse of King Tut. Doom, for sure. If only he'd stick to what he's good at—writing—and leave the how-toing to someone who really knows how to.

"Hey, Katie! Come here! You're gonna love this!" Dad opened my door and grabbed my arm. He dragged me to a hideous snarl of dead-looking branches which arched over the pathway leading to the front door. "You'll never guess what this is."

"I can't stand the suspense."

"It's a kissing hedge!" Dad wagged his forefinger at me. "I'm keeping a sharp lookout on you and all your boyfriends."

"Dad, cut it out." Fat chance any of those rich guys would kiss me when they found out I lived in this disaster area. Sweet fifteen and never been kissed. Well, not kissed enough. My first real romance had been nipped in the bud when we'd moved. From the looks of it, I might as well kiss my kissing days goodbye.

Mom cleared her throat. "Ah, it really does have...potential, dear." I glared at her. "Well, it could use some work, but that's the whole idea. Isn't it, Kate?'' There was an unmistakable challenge in her voice.

"Oh yeah, sure," I mumbled.

"You wait. This house'll be so gorgeous it'll knock you out. Imagine next summer, it's cleaned up, shimmering like a fairy tale castle above Blue Heron Lake..." Dad's voice trailed off, as if that vision were too much even for him. The four of us stood there a moment, staring at the place. When we'd left Colorado the sun had been out, the sky blue, the whole world bright with newly fallen snow. It had been two days after Christmas, and had looked the way Christmastime is supposed to look.

But here—here everything was damp, dreary. It was too warm for snow, but a chilly rain had sifted down nonstop ever since we'd crossed the Cascade Mountains. Not even a good, hard, honest rain. More like dense drizzle. Ghostly puffs of mist hovered in midair and clung to the top of a turret which loomed at the rear of the house. Fir trees sagged and dripped. An evil-looking mass of brambles bristled by the road, snaked up trees and threatened to devour the driveway.

"Oregonians don't tan, they rust," Dad had joked when he'd returned to Colorado to tell us about the house he'd be renovating for his next how-to book. Mildew is more like it. I looked down to find a huge slug undulating up the toe of my sneaker. "Oh, yuck!" I shook my foot violently until the slug flopped off.

Dad was struggling with the front door. It was one of those massive oak numbers, standard equipment on your basic haunted house. He tried to open it in the usual way, but it wouldn't budge. He gave a mighty shove. The door abruptly lunged open, catapulting him into the house. Dad's feet shot out from under him and he spread-eagled on the floor. Cyrano waddled inside and licked his face.

Dad picked himself up, dusting off his pants. "It sticks."

Giggles burst from Amy and me like air escaping a balloon. "No kidding," I said.

But inside, I didn't feel much like laughing. It was dark, even after Dad flipped on the lights. A sharp, musty smell prickled my nose. Ancient, floral-print wallpaper curled away from the baseboards and crumbled in the corners. You could see outlines of where furniture had been because the paper behind it hadn't got as dingy as the rest. A steep staircase curved up in one corner, and spider webs trailed down from massive beams. I shivered. This place gave me the creeps.

I felt a tug at my sweater and reached down to close Amy's hand in mine.

Dad strode across the creaking floorboards to a room at the back of the house. "They say the doctor who built this house was having dinner with his wife here one night in 1928. For some reason they got up from the table. They left their meal half-eaten." Dad paused dramatically. "And never came back."

"Why not?" I asked.

"No one seems to know for sure. Afterward, Dr. Mathieson moved to Portland and set up practice there. They say he never set foot in this house again. Didn't sell it, either. He just hired someone to shut it down, with practically everything still in it, and do occasional maintenance."

"You mean nobody's lived here since 1928? No wonder it's such a..." I caught Mom's look. "So interesting."

"Actually, the place has been rented out several times. But no one ever stayed long."

"What about the woman?"

"What woman?"

"The doctor's wife. Did she go to Portland, too?"

"Uh, no. No one seems to know what she did. Local legend has it she—just disappeared that night."

A tingly feeling crept up my shoulders and neck. "Did he murder her?" I hoped so. There's nothing like a good murder to take your mind off your troubles.

"No, of course not." Dad looked irritated, as though he wished he'd never brought up the subject. "Anyway, that's probably where all that 'haunted' nonsense came from."

The way the house looks might just possibly have something to do with it, I thought. But I was Exercising Restraint, so all I said was, "Who told you it was haunted, anyway?"

"It's not really haunted. The real estate agent said it had that reputation. Probably a bunch of kids with overactive imaginations. But we got a honey of a deal on this old place. Lakefront property is golden in this town. After Dr. Mathieson died, no one else made a decent offer..."

"Because it's haunted?" I love to bait Dad.

"*It's not haunted!* No, because of the, uh, deferred maintenance items."

Deferred maintenance items? Now there's a dignified phrase. Meaning the place is a wreck. But I kept my mouth shut. Restraint.

"Hey, I've got a surprise for you girls, but I want to show you the backyard first."

We all thrashed through the dusty drapes and came out on a small deck. It hung way out over a hill so steep, you'd almost call it a cliff. Beyond the iron railing, a trail zigzagged down the bramble-covered hillside until it ended, far below, at the lake.

To get to the trail you had to go down this skinny, slippery wrought-iron stairway. There was a twenty-foot drop to the nearest solid ground, and beyond that, more bramble-covered hillside, and beyond that, water, dark gray and opaque.

"Charming," I said, turning to go inside.

"Hey, Katie, where're you going?" Dad asked. "C'mon. I want you to see the lake up close."

"I'll pass."

"Come on," coaxed Dad. "You can do it. Just hang on the railing, there you go..." and he shooed me onto the stairway. My chest tightened as I looked down toward the water, so I focused on my feet. I'd have been okay if only Amy hadn't appointed herself my personal shadow lately. Before Mom or Dad could stop her, she launched herself down the steps, wailing, "Katie! Wait for me! Wait!"

I felt a jolt at the back of my knees when Amy ricocheted off me. There was a shrill, grating sound as the railing I held tore loose from its post and swung out over the cliff. I lurched off the stairway, gripping the loose rail for dear life.

The ground wobbled crazily beneath me. I shut my eyes and saw dark water. Through a dull, rushing noise, dim voices called my name. Dad's. Amy's. Mom's. The rushing noise grew louder, broke over the voices, roared inside my head. And the water rose again, the old nightmare, up past my mouth, my nose, closing over my eyes.

"Katie! Give me your hand! Katie!"

Dad's voice cut through the roar in my head. I opened my eyes, saw his hand in front of me. I reached out and felt him clamp my wrist, felt myself swinging in close to the stairway. Sideways, knees and elbows gripping the steps, I hauled myself up.

"What happened? Why didn't you give me your hand?" Dad demanded.

I lay numb for a moment, listening to my heartbeat and to the quick, rhythmic huffs of Dad's breath. My whole body felt like rubber, except my knees and elbow, which throbbed from banging against the metal steps. "I did," I said. Slowly I crawled back up to the deck.

"Kate. Are you all right?" Mom asked.

"But why did you take so long? What happened? Katie..."

"I'll tell you what happened. You brought me *here*." I rubbed my elbow and tried to push down the rage building up inside me, tried to stop the words from coming. But they just came bursting out. "First you make me leave the friends I've known all my life. Then you move me here to this slum and expect me to fit right into a town full of rich kids. In the middle of the school year! Now it turns out this place is a death trap. I could have broken both legs! I could have been killed, and you don't even care! It's all your fault, Dad. You and that—that book of yours."

"That's enough!" Mom's voice cut through the heavy air.

Typical. He practically gets me killed, and there she goes, protecting him again. I made for the house, my fingernails burning into my palms, my pulse still pounding in my ears. Drat him! I hadn't had that old water nightmare since I was little, but this place had reactivated it in less than ten minutes.

Amy scrambled after me.

"I think Cyrano is having a problem," I said.

Our pug dog stood just inside the doorway. Violent shudders rippled across his fat body, punctuated by thunderous snorts. I picked him up. "We'll steam him out in the bathroom."

We found the upstairs bathroom without much trouble. I turned on the hot water in the sink full blast. The bathtub was one of those old-fashioned deals with claws for legs. I twisted the tap. It came off in my hand.

"Oh, great." Water, water everywhere. First I flash on the time I almost drowned in the ocean when I was three years old and now this. "Just great."

Amy snuggled into my lap as fog filled the room. I scratched behind Cyrano's ears. "You all right, fella?" He snorted. His nose was so squashed-looking, it's no wonder he had problems. A little too much excitement, then—snort attack! All of a sudden he could hardly breathe. But the old steam treatment worked every time.

The snort level had already dropped a couple of decibels. Now Cyrano sounded almost normal. For him, that is. In some ways, Cyrano was more like a pig than a dog. Squashed pig snout. Curly pig tail. Bulging pig fat.

"Presenting—The World's Ugliest Dog. Otherwise known as The World's Prettiest Pig." The familiar laughing voice echoed in my mind. Becky. Just thinking about Becky made me feel lonely. Becky Jonston and I had grown up together, best friends, never guessing that someday she would suddenly turn into a Barbie doll look-alike while I cultivated my feet, legs and nose. At last count, my feet were size ten, my legs put me over the five-foot-ten mark and my nose looked like Pinocchio flunking a lie detector test. Meanwhile, the parts I wanted to cultivate reminded me of a book I once read on Alaska: *The Vast, Undeveloped Territory.*

Actually, I never minded much. Not in Colorado. People knew me there. They knew my family. I had friends. Especially Becky. I'd had a few dates, and lately practically even a boyfriend.

But here, now what did I have? How would all those rich kids in the town of Blue Heron see me? No beauty. No money. A father who demolishes our home and personal possessions for a living. A mother who prefers Bunsen burners to the kind on top of the stove. A snot-nosed sister wearing muddy shoes. The World's Ugliest Dog in midsnort attack. A house that would give Dracula goose bumps.

Face it, I was an oddball, and my family was positively weird. If that ghost ever got a good look at the Hardin family, *it* would be the one scared off. I'd just like to see the look on that ghost's face if it came in here right now.

I started as the floor outside the bathroom door creaked loudly. "Hello?" said a voice, a voice I'd never heard before in my life. "May I come in?"

Chapter Two

With all that steam fogging up the room, the apparition at the door did have a ghostly look to it. But this
ghost knew how to dress. She had on a rose-colored
sweater that looked all fluffy, like the angora one Dad
gave Mom on their fifteenth wedding anniversary. The
ghost also wore a pair of black pants I'd seen adver-
tised in *Mademoiselle*. I was waiting for Sears to come
out with a cheaper version. Then came the hot pink
shoes with little cutouts and rhinestones. Esprit, no
doubt. No self-respecting Blue Heron ghost would be
caught dead in an off brand.

"Uh, hi." I stood, and Amy slid from my lap.

"Hi. I'm Jessamyn Winter," said the apparition,
flashing a smile that could only be called dazzling.
"My mother sent me over with a fondue. Your dad
said you were here, so I came up." She tossed her

head. Blond hair flared out around her in a silky fan. She looked like a shampoo commercial.

"I'm Kate Hardin," I said, running a hand through my hair. As if that would help. "This is my sister, Amy. And, uh, Cyrano."

By now I was pretty certain this was a real girl, not a ghost. For one thing, I'd never heard of a ghost delivering fondue for her mother. Besides, up close Jessamyn looked pretty substantial. Parts of her, anyway. Where I was The Vast Undeveloped Territory, Jessamyn was The Land of Plenty. Everywhere else, she was tiny.

Cyrano chugged toward Jessamyn, snorted, drooled, flopped his tail from side to side. I watched, helpless, as a drop of drool spattered perilously close to the hot pink Esprits. Jessamyn took one slow step back, then a faster one. She was in full retreat when Dad broke in.

"Well, girls. I see you found each other." Dad scooped up Cyrano and held the dog close to Jessamyn's face. "Making friends, are you?" he joked, oblivious to Jessamyn's repulsed look. Cyrano snorted. "You okay now, fella?"

"He's better." I turned to Jessamyn. "His nose gets clogged sometimes, and we have to steam up the air so he can breathe."

"Oh."

"Well." Dad looked from me to Jessamyn, as if waiting for us to break out in scintillating conversation. We didn't. "So. Why don't you turn off the water in the tub, Katie? Then we'll all go up and take a look at that surprise I told you about."

"I can't." I held up the broken tap handle.

"Oh." Dad leaned over the tub and fiddled with the spigot, but to no avail.

"Um, I'd better go now," said Jessamyn.

"Nonsense, Jessie. We'll go see that surprise right now. You'll love it. Amy, you go down and ask your mom to get you a wrench. Then meet us upstairs."

At the end of the hallway we climbed a narrow staircase to a small, octagonal room. The turret. Gray light filtered in through dirty windows on all eight walls but one. There stood a huge, oval mirror. An etched design twined around the mirror's edges, branching into delicate, lacing tendrils at the top and bottom. The rest of the room was bare except for lots of dust and two ratty old trunks.

Dad, eager as Ali Baba open-sesameing the cave, fumbled with the latch on one trunk. Dust and a musty odor exhaled like bad breath as the lid creaked, then wobbled open. "Ta da!" Dad pulled out something white and rumpled. An old bedspread? It unfurled in dusty folds. No, it was a cape. A full-length velvet cape. White fur nestled at the neckline.

"White fox," whispered Jessamyn, touching her cheek to the collar. Dad handed her the cape, and she held it up to herself in front of the mirror. "It's beautiful."

Dad excused himself to go downstairs; Jessamyn and I bent together over the trunk. I found a navy-blue dress with a row of tiny buttons and a sash way down low on the hips. The hem hit just below my knees. It reminded me of the flapper dresses I'd seen in pictures of the Roaring Twenties.

"Wool jersey," said Jessamyn, fingering the dress. She pulled out a coat cut like a bathrobe and covered with short, light brown fur. "Goatskin. Sheared goatskin."

I didn't have much experience with expensive clothes, but I could tell right off these weren't cheap. One dress was thick with embroidery, another trimmed in shimmering curlicues of braid. Silk, Jessamyn said. There was a lot of silk. At least a half dozen silk dresses and a dozen silk scarves. Plus lots and lots of shoes. One pair had shiny gold trim; on another, silver threads wove through a sort of tapestry material. We opened the second trunk; inside were boxes of small, close-fitting hats.

I tried one on. "A flapper hat!"

"Cloche," said Jessamyn. She pronounced it "klosh."

"What?"

"Cloche. A cloche hat. That's what they called them in the twenties."

"You sure know a lot about clothes."

"I love clothes. I'm going to be a fashion designer."

Ordinarily I'd be embarrassed playing dress-up with a kid my age. But Jessamyn's professional interest made it seem okay. We flung coats and capes over our shoulders, slipped into shoes and tilted hats on our heads. I made a dumb face in the mirror, and pretty soon we were both posing outrageously, giggling like crazy.

"This wench is heavy!" Amy burst into the room, dropped the wrench and flopped on the floor.

"Amy! Amy, you up there?" Footsteps sounded on the stairs, then Dad poked his head through the doorway. "There you are. C'mon help me with the wrench."

"Hey, Dad. Did these belong to the doctor's wife?" I asked.

"Sure did. But they're yours now. They were found here in the house—in the attic—but they're not worth much anymore. Damaged, most of them. Yellow stains or little holes or... here, like this." He held up a dress with an intricate pattern worked in tiny beads. The fabric had shredded near the shoulders. "So I made them part of the deal when I bought the place."

"I wonder what she looked like," I mused, trying to imagine the elegant lady who wore these clothes long ago.

"I'll show you." Dad rummaged under the hat boxes and came up with a worn, velvet-covered photo album. The pages inside looked crumbly; the photos had a yellow cast. "Here's Elise Mathieson, the wife of the doctor who had this house built. Here's Dr. Mathieson."

The woman in the picture had linked arms with two men. Her head was thrown back in laughter; both men were smiling at her. The man who wasn't the doctor wore a white suit and hat. He looked like Robert Redford.

"Who's the other man?"

"I don't know. Probably one of Portland's high society crowd. From what I understand, the Mathiesons mingled with the upper crust."

Elise's hairdo and clothes looked old-fashioned, but you could tell she'd been beautiful. And self-confident. And popular. And rich. Everything I wasn't. I sighed. I wonder what happened to her. Had the doctor murdered her?

"Hey, Katie, look at me!" Amy tottered around the room in a pair of high heels, blinded by a purple hat.

"Cute, Amy. Real cute."

"What a lovely young lady you are!" Dad hefted Amy to his shoulders and picked up the wrench. "Come help the horsey fix the bathroom faucet."

"Giddap!" Amy and the "horsey" galloped down the stairs.

Jessamyn and I paged silently through the album for a while. Most of the pictures were of glamorous-looking adults leading the good life, or at least what passed for the good life back then. The only kid in the batch was this sad-faced boy about Amy's age. He wore one of those ridiculous sailor suits they dressed kids in. A dirty bandage hung from one knee. He looked lost.

"You must be really brave to live here," Jessamyn said.

"Why, because of the ghost?" I tried to keep my voice light.

"No, I wasn't thinking of her. What I meant was, the house isn't exactly, well . . ."

"Yeah, it's a dump, isn't it?"

"I didn't . . ."

"Look, I know it is. We're here to humor my dad. He writes books and his next one is on fixing up this place."

"Oh. You're braver than I am. I couldn't stand it."

Me neither, I thought. I bit my lip and turned another page in the album. A huge photograph of Elise sort of half-smiled up at me, teasingly.

"You said 'her.' You've heard about the ghost?"

"Everybody has. The kids around here think this is their private haunted house. The younger kids, I mean. Like my brother. Some of them were even mad when they found out you were coming. It's like it belongs to the neighborhood or something. Plus, they all want to find the treasure."

"The treasure?"

"Yeah. Some people say there's a treasure hidden on the property. Though with all the kids snooping around, they'd have found it by now, for sure. Of course, I'm glad you're here," she added graciously. "Those kids are a pain, with their dumb ghost stories."

"Wow," I said. "A treasure." And then, "I take it the ghost is supposed to be Elise Mathieson."

"Yeah. The doctor's wife."

"So why is she haunting—I mean, supposedly?"

"Well, the story goes that the doctor's cruel to her and she falls in love with another man. She's supposed to run away with him one night. So she packs up her money and jewelry and stuff—maybe that's the treasure, who knows?—and waits practically all night with a yellow lantern down by the lake for him to pick her up in his boat. But he never comes. So she kills herself. Dumb. Anyway, that's why the ghost carries a yellow lantern, supposedly. Waiting for her lover to come."

"Unrequited love and all that."

"I guess so. Not too bright."

"Why do you say that?"

"If you want a guy bad enough, you'll find a way to get him. Especially if you're pretty, like she was."

"Oh." This was news to me. "Did they ever find bones or anything?"

"No. It's just a story." Jessamyn looked at her watch, one of those sleek gold jobs with no numbers. "Now I've really got to go. Hey, but why don't you come for dinner tomorrow night?"

"I'd love to! Um, but I'd better check with my parents."

"You really have to ask?"

I nodded.

"Then ask about Friday night, too. I'm having a big New Year's Eve thing at my house. Tons of kids from school are coming. That'll be good for you. You need to know some people."

"That would be great." I tried to act cool, as if I got invited to big New Year's Eve things all the time. As if my parents let me go to big New Year's Eve things all the time.

But surprisingly, they did. In fact, they both looked pleased I'd been invited. They didn't even ask any stupid questions like who's going to be there, what are you going to do, what time will you be back, et cetera, et cetera. And they said okay to dinner, too.

"Super!" Jessamyn actually sounded happy as we headed for the door. "See you tomorrow night."

For the next several hours I was too busy to think about Jessamyn or dinner at her house or the New Year's thing with tons of rich kids. We finished unloading the car, scrubbed down the kitchen cupboards, then filled them with the food and utensils we'd brought. The movers weren't coming until the next day, so we didn't have too much to put away. Mom had brought plenty of cleaning stuff, though. By the end of the day, most of the loose dirt had been swept, mopped or scrubbed into submission, and a hundred spiders were out looking for new homes.

For dinner we had a cheese fondue picnic over a Bunsen burner on the living room floor.

"Elegant," I pronounced.

"Don't we have anything to *eat*?" Dad asked.

"Yucchy," Amy said.

So we finished up at Burger King. I took a good look at all the other kids there, but mostly they were nothing special, just like ordinary Colorado kids.

Back at the house we rolled out our sleeping bags. Mom tucked Amy into hers, then she and Dad went downstairs. I hung around in my room for a while, but there was nothing to do, so I climbed the stairs to the turret room.

The single bare light bulb hollowed out a narrow cone of light in the middle of the room. I picked up the photo album and sat in the bright spot on the floor. "Elise." I said the name out loud. Elise at a party, Elise on the lake in a boat. Elise clowning around in one of those old-fashioned swim suits. Elise holding up a cocktail glass for a toast. Beautiful, charming Elise. Elise was always in focus; other people blurred around her. They seemed to hover near her, as though for warmth. Even as they smiled, their eyes, when you looked close, seemed to be watching Elise.

I sighed and put down the album. I bet the bathtub never broke when Elise lived here.

The fox-trimmed cloak was draped over one of the trunks. I pulled it around me, then slipped my bare feet into the shoes with the silver threads. They fit perfectly. In the mirror in the dim room, I didn't look my usual gangly self. When I held my head a certain way I looked almost elegant. Almost beautiful. I imagined laughing and linking arms with two good-looking guys. I was witty. Charming. Rich. I dug through the trunk for a feathered fan I'd seen earlier. I fanned myself gaily. My nose was well-proportioned, my family was not weird, my dog did not snort. My entire life and everything around me reflected dignity and taste.

I stared out into the darkness. Lights winked on the other side of the lake, blurred through patches of fog. Maybe there was something magic about this place. Jessamyn seemed to want me around. And here, in this room, in these clothes, life seemed full of exciting possibilities.

A rush of expectation surged through me as I thought about the New Year's Eve party. I spun around, the cloak unfurling about me.

Suddenly, I froze. There, down by the lake, was a light. Not still and far off like the others. This light was on our side of the lake, and it was moving, moving up toward the house. It wasn't a flashlight, either, not white and sharp and slanting. No, it glowed hazy yellow, like—like a yellow lantern.

Chapter Three

E lise," I whispered.

The yellow light stopped. It sort of hovered around in one spot, as if listening, listening for... for what? Then it drifted, zigzagged, slowly up the hill, coming closer and closer.

A delicious chill thrilled up my spine and tingled at the base of my neck. I drew the cape close about me, stared hard into the night. The darkness, at first a flat pitch black, gradually clarified into vague silhouettes: a boulder, tree branches, a tangle of vine, a shadow beside the light. Whether it were a man or woman, I couldn't tell.

All at once a ferocious yapping ruptured the silence. Cyrano. The light plunged left and kept going, past where our property ended and back downhill toward the lake. It faded, dimmer and dimmer, then suddenly, eerily, disappeared altogether. No, not quite. For a while a glow so faint that I could barely make it out, a sort of halo, floated to the left. Then it vanished, too. It was as if the ghost—or whatever it was— had jumped into the lake and swum away under water.

"Wow." I lowered myself to the floor, my legs feeling shaky and unreliable. Downstairs, a door clicked open. I heard Mom scolding Cyrano, then the door thudding shut, then a distant murmur of voices, Mom's and Dad's.

The whole incident couldn't have lasted more than a couple of minutes, but it felt as though I'd just snapped out of a two-week trance. I took a couple of deep breaths. In through the nose, out through the mouth. That's a trick I learned from one of Dad's books, *How to Defuse Deadly Stress Bombs—Starting Now!* I didn't know if seeing your first ghost qualified as a Deadly Stress Bomb, but the deep breathing helped.

If it really was a ghost. Highly dubious. But still, a possibility. I wondered what Mom and Dad would say when I told them. *Hey, guys, just saw old Elise and the yellow lantern haunting the backyard.* Sure, Kate. *Yeah, then she hustled on down the hill and vanished underwater.* Uh-huh. Probably they'd write off the whole thing to my overactive imagination—that ever-popular term parents use to pooh-pooh stuff their kids saw and they missed.

I got weakly to my feet, put away the cape and shoes and stumbled to my room. Forget about that dumb ghost, I told myself as I crawled into my sleeping bag. I'll deal with it tomorrow. The last thought that lodged in my mind before sleep flowed in was to wonder why a ghost would run from a fat pug dog.

Something wet was dragging across my face.

"Cyrano! Oh, yuck! Cyrano, stop licking me!"

"Hieeeee!" A chilling scream reverberated inside my skull as forty-two pounds of attacking four-year-old landed on my stomach.

"Oh, jeez! Ouch! Okay! I'm getting up."

I extracted myself from the squirming tangle of dog, sister and sleeping bag, then rummaged through my suitcase for a clean shirt. In the gray morning light, that ghost business of last night seemed absurd. There must be some completely logical explanation. And the bit about the underwater glow—I grinned and shook my head as I pulled on my jeans. It probably had been my overactive imagination.

Yeah, the old overactive imagination had been working overtime last night, I thought, tugging a brush through my hair. Then I'd imagined I was some kind of teenage sex goddess. This morning, no way. Slobbering pugs and karateing four-year-olds have a way of busting up your fantasies. So do mirrors. I checked out the reflection. Same old face. Same old hair. Same old me. Oh, well.

"You are taking forever and forever!" Amy grabbed my legs from behind and butted me toward the stairs.

In the kitchen I poured dry dog food into a bowl for Cyrano and dry cereal into bowls for Amy and me.

"Another day, another bowl of Bran Krispins," said Dad, winking at Amy and me as he poured his.

"Look here!" Mom grabbed the cereal box and pointed to the nutrition label. "One hundred percent of your minimum daily requirement. It's a miracle of modern chemistry!"

"Uh-huh. Speaking of chemistry, Jeanne, when did you say you start classes? Week after next, isn't it?"

"Yes. But I start work at the lab next Monday." Mom smiled as she stirred freeze-dried coffee crystals into two mugs of steaming water. "After all these years, I'm finally getting paid for lab work. Even if it is only a graduate assistant's salary."

"I saw something last night," I said between bites of Bran Krispins.

"I'll have my doctorate in three years, and then we'll be able to—what did you say, Kate?"

"I saw something last night. A light in the back-yard."

Mom gave a little jerk, and coffee spilled down the side of her mug. She and Dad both stared at me, then looked quickly at each other.

"What kind of light?" Dad asked.

"How should I know? Yellow. It was coming up the path from the lake."

"Why didn't you tell us then?" Dad's voice was sharp, which surprised me. It hardly ever is.

"It was gone before I could have got to you. I'm sure it's nothing important. Maybe my overactive imagination or something, with all that talk about Elise and haunting and stuff."

"If you ever see anything like that again, tell us right away! Do you understand? You too, Amy," said Dad.

"Okay, okay. No need to get all worked up." I shuffled to the sink and rinsed out my bowl. "All right if I check out the backyard this morning, till the movers come?"

Dad seemed about to say something else, but he looked at Mom instead.

"Go ahead," Mom said, finally, "as long as you take Amy and Cyrano with you. And don't touch that railing. Dad put it back yesterday but it'll break again if you lean on it. And be back by noon. The movers are due then. We'll need your help."

The air outside felt heavy with water, but you couldn't really call it rain. A milky fog spilled out over the lake and pooled around low tree branches. Maybe I could find some clue out here, if I only knew where to look.

"Hold my hand?" Amy tugged at my slicker as we crossed the deck to the wrought-iron stairway.

"All right, but be careful this time." I swallowed, pushing back the remembered rush of water. "Hey, Ames! Don't hold that railing. Just me."

Amy and I scooted down the stairs on our rear ends; Cyrano hurtled past.

We set off down the switchbacks, down stone steps and gravel stretches. The steep hill had been landscaped as a sort of rock garden. Although garden is too nice a word for anything so completely out of control. Ivy and brambles crisscrossed the path, strangled tree trunks and smothered huge rocks. In some places the ivy had died, leaving hard cages of root and vine where boulders crouched like criminals.

Amy let go of my hand; she and Cyrano romped on ahead. What really got me was the moss. They say

Eskimos have two dozen words for snow; I wondered
how many Oregonians have for moss. Your basic deep
green, medium-pile variety carpeted rocks and upholstered low tree branches. A kind of slimy, greenish-
yellow stuff coated other rocks. High in the bare
branches of trees, the moss—fungus?—got all lacy
and pastel green. Entire trees appeared to have broken out in doilies.

"Amy! Wait up, would you!"

Amy, near the bottom of the hill, sent me a look of
pure mutiny, then darted toward the lake. "I'll beat!
I'll beat!" she screamed gleefully.

"Oh, no you won't," I muttered through clenched
teeth as I took off down the hill. I grabbed the back of
her slicker just as she reached the edge of the lake.
"Don't run near the water!"

"Why not?"

"You might slip and fall in. And you can't swim."

"Then you would jump in and save me."

"Don't be so sure. I hate water."

"You would, too."

I sighed. "Just don't run, okay?"

From here I could tell this was one weird lake.
Docks and boat houses jutted out all over the place.
Which was okay, except they stood at least four feet
above water level. You could see all the little support
beams underneath. Plus, this dark gray band ran
along the inside of the lake bed just under the docks
and boat houses, right where you'd expect water level
to be. If I didn't know better, I'd say it was low tide.

"Stand here a minute, Amy. I want to see something."

I crouched on my hands and knees near the edge of the lake and looked down. Water. Quickly, I glanced away and found the gray band; I touched it and rubbed my fingers together. It felt slimy. Then I noticed something really strange a few yards to my right. Steps. A flight of concrete steps leading straight down into the water.

"Lose something?"

I almost fell into the lake.

The first thing I saw was a pair of gym shoes which looked as if they'd been through a marathon. The original marathon. Clambering to my feet, I took in the blue jeans—well, formerly blue. At our house, they'd be well into their next reincarnation as dust rags. Ditto the army jacket. At last I came eye-to-eye with a freckle-faced guy with ears like Alfred E. Neuman's.

"I didn't scare you, did I?" He didn't sound the least bit repentant.

"Oh, no. I always jump like that for no reason."

The eyes studied me, light gray, almost colorless. I had the uneasy feeling this guy could see into my mind and was amused at what he found there.

"You really ought to get your front door fixed," he said, finally.

"What?"

"Your dad bruised his shin trying to open it. It sticks."

"We just got here yesterday," I said, then mentally kicked myself. I didn't have to make excuses to him.

"What's your name? I'm four," piped up Amy.

"Kirk O'Brien. You must be Amy."

"Amy Alexandria Hardin." Having exhausted her repertoire of social graces, Amy ducked behind me and did her famous boa constrictor imitation around my legs.

Kirk knelt beside her. "Amy, do you like chocolate-chip cookies?"

"Yum!"

"My mom made some for you guys. I left them up at your house."

"Yum!"

"She's cute." Kirk straightened. "My mom thinks it's her sacred obligation to load up the neighbors with refined sugar and saturated fat."

I laughed grudgingly. "That's okay by me."

"So where'd you see this ghost last night?"

I never have figured out exactly what hackles are, but I definitely felt mine rise. "Now wait a minute. I saw a light. I never said anything about . . ."

"Would you relax? Your dad told me all about it and wanted to know if I knew anything about the local ghost."

"Well? Do you?"

"No. Only . . ."

"Only what?"

"First tell me what you saw."

Oh, please, I thought. "Just a light in the backyard."

"Yellow, your dad said."

"Uh, yeah."

"Kind of hazy, no doubt."

"What do you mean, hazy? Of course it was hazy; the fog out here was a mile thick!"

"Ah, the infamous hazy yellow lantern."

"Now, look here..." I began.

"Calm down. I believe you." He was studying me again. "I do, really."

He didn't seem to be laughing at me. "Anyway, the infamous yellow lantern wasn't the weird part," I said.

"What was?"

"Well, our dog barked, then the light went over that way. Then it disappeared, except I could still see a glow, kind of like"—I mumbled the last part, afraid Kirk would laugh after all "—it was moving away under water. Or something."

Kirk didn't laugh. "Where did you say that was?"

"That way." I pointed across the steep, rocky hillside to the left of our house. "By the lake."

Kirk stared at me again with those uncanny eyes. "Come on," he said at last, and struck out across the hillside.

"Where to?"

"I want to show you something." He didn't even slow down.

"I'm not going anywhere until you tell me what you said you were going to tell me. About—you know—ghosts."

"I'll tell you on the way," Kirk yelled over his shoulder. I stood a moment, then grabbed Amy's hand and scrambled after him.

"Some of the kids around here weren't too crazy about your taking over the local haunted house," Kirk said while Amy and I puffed behind. "Transylvania-on-the-lake. They used to sneak in there and hunt for treasure and spook themselves out. I wouldn't put it past them to...oh gawd!"

I whirled around. "What!"

"That's the ugliest dog I've ever seen!"

Ever the intrepid watchdog, Cyrano waddled up to Kirk and drooled on his shoe. The dog snorted in wild abandon as Kirk scratched behind his ears.

"Hey, boy, what's your name?"

"It's Cyrano."

"Cyrano? As in Cyrano de Bergerac? The French guy with the big nose?"

I colored. Kirk laughed aloud as he turned and set off across the hillside.

"You were saying, about the kids . . ." I prompted, trotting to keep up, dragging Amy behind me.

"Right. I wouldn't be surprised if they decided to do some haunting themselves. Maybe to scare off the nasty usurpers. You, that is. Or maybe because now they have a captive audience."

"Us, that is."

"Right."

"So you think it was the kids."

"That's the logical explanation."

I shrugged.

Kirk gave me another looking-through-you-look. "The lady not only sees ghosts, she believes in them, too."

"Not necessarily. I just like to look at all the possibilities."

"Hmm. Madam Skeptic."

"That's me. So would you mind telling me exactly where we're going? I'm feeling skeptical about racing around on the side of this cliff."

Kirk looked surprised, then slowed down a little. "We're going to take a look at where your ghost disappeared into the lake."

"Why, to look for telltale ripples?"

"There's no water over there."

"What?"

"Didn't you know? The lake gets drained part way every winter so people can fix their docks and retaining walls. It's still going down. This year they're draining out more water than usual, to fix a sewer pipe or something."

So that was it. No wonder it looked like low tide. "How long's the water going to be out?" Just my luck to move into a home with a panoramic view of a giant mud puddle.

"End of this month."

"So how come there's no water over there? There's still plenty by our house. It's only down about four feet."

"Over there it's shallower. It's a bay, off the main lake."

"So the ghost, or whoever, wouldn't have made any ripples at all. It would have made . . ."

"You got it."

The hill had leveled off now, and the going got easier as we approached the bay. Kirk was right. The lake edge dropped off only a couple of feet into the lake bed. At the bottom of the bed was mud, not water. A sluggish stream ran through the center of the bay; hacked-off tree stumps dotted the mud. Kirk, now several feet ahead of me, stopped and pointed.

"There they are," he said as though he'd known all along.

Running along the mud near the shore, they were impossible to miss.

Footprints.

Chapter Four

The weirdest things flash through your mind sometimes. When I first set eyes on those footprints, all I could think of was this book I read where a ghost supposedly tracks wet footprints across the deck of a boat.

"So much for ghosts," said Kirk. "It's kids, like I said."

"Not necessarily." I told him about the book.

"That's ridiculous." Kirk shook his head and swung down onto the lake bed. Cyrano dove in after. "Here's another possibility. That yellow light you saw is a fig newton of your imagination."

"You sound just like my parents, you know that? And my imagination hasn't even got started yet. It could have been a robber, casing out the place. Or an anthropologist discovering traces of some ancient Indian civilization. Or a Russian spy, or a treasure hunter or a . . ."

"It's kids, and you know it." Kirk squatted by one of the prints. I stepped gingerly onto the lake bed, then helped Amy down. My feet sank into the mud.

"Looks like they were all made by the same guy," Kirk said. "Same pattern. Hiking boots, I bet. They do look kind of big for a kid, but—wait a minute. Come here."

"Why?"

"Put your foot there."

Feeling stupid, I set down my size-ten foot next to one of the prints. It was almost the same length. "See!" Kirk was triumphant. "It was a kid. A kid with big feet!"

"Gee, thanks," I said. Kirk ignored me and took off in hot pursuit of clues. Out in the middle of the bay a flock of ducks swam in the brown stream, their shapes vague, their gabblings muted by fog. Occasional rock piles scabbed over the mud; pools of mist vaporized into nothingness in the distance. The drained lake looked like some alien landscape, made more bizarre by snatches of the familiar. A rusty beer can. A Mr. Goodbar wrapper. A Day-Glo orange buoy with the word slow painted on it, stranded in a puddle.

I set out after Kirk along the edge of the bay, following the footprints. Amy ran behind, screaming, "Help! Quicksand! Oh, help!" She sank to her ankles in mud, pulled out one foot, tripped, fell, splat, all the while giggling and squealing in ecstasy. Cyrano took off after the ducks, which scattered, quacking madly.

Kirk had stopped near a paved bridge which arched over a narrow part of the bay. "Here's where he got out," he said when I caught up to him.

I nodded. The prints ended here. We stood awhile, not saying anything. I felt like the Man with the X-Ray Eyes or something, staring beyond the surface, seeing things that were supposed to be covered by water. The absurdly elongated legs of the docks. The shocking nakedness of an island beneath its sudden thatch of ferns and trees. I pictured the lake rising, seeking its natural level, and my throat tightened the way it always does when I'm around big bodies of water. Then Amy was tugging at my sleeve, saying, "I wanna go home."

"Me too, Ames. We'll... Where's your shoe?"

"It got lost."

There followed a squishy search of the lake bed during which we totally obliterated what was left of the footprints. Kirk finally discovered the shoe capsized in a mud puddle.

"What's your mom going to say when she sees, ah..." he nodded at Amy, who looked as though someone had held her by the hair and dipped her in a vat of chocolate.

"Mom always says a clean kid is a bored kid, and she's not raising any bored children. Anyway, dirt comes off with soap and water, so we don't worry about it. Right, Amy?"

"We don't worry about dirt," Amy informed Kirk.

"If you say so." Kirk shrugged. "Where's de Bergerac?"

Still terrorizing ducks. "Cyrano! Here, boy! Come! Cyrano!" I called. He refused, so I had to chase him down and lug him back across the lake bed.

Actually, it's a good thing the movers were there when we got home. In spite of what I'd said to Kirk, Mom would probably have worked up a lecture if she'd had the chance. Amy was a mess. So was Cyrano. After Kirk left, Amy and I took off our shoes and sneaked up to the bathroom with Cyrano. I stripped Amy and wrapped her clothes in a towel. Then I cranked on the tap with the wrench Dad had left, and got into some serious scrubbing.

The rest of the day I spent keeping Amy and Cyrano out of trouble, unpacking boxes and putting things away. We got so busy, I totally forgot about the footprints. It was six o'clock before I had time to wonder what to wear to Jessamyn's house. So I picked out a skirt and a sweater, pulled a brush through my hair and hoped I looked acceptable.

It was already dark out when I left. Dad had made me take a flashlight, which I'd thought was dumb, but now I was glad. What with all the trees around here, you could hardly even see any stars. I thought of the light last night and walked faster. Three houses to the left. There it was.

The house loomed above me as I stepped up to the front door. But Jessamyn's house didn't loom in the same way ours loomed. Not spookily. Magnificently. It was one of those modern places with all the wood and glass and vaulted ceilings and skylights. The kind of house that sends real estate agents into paroxysms of purple prose.

The doorbell, not content with a modest ding dong, struck up the third verse just as a pale blond woman appeared at the door.

"Hello?" she asked, uncertainly.

"I . . . I'm Kate Hardin. Jessamyn said . . ."

"Oh, Jessie's friend." The woman opened the door wide enough for me to step through. Physically, she looked a lot like Jessamyn: the eyes, the hair, the shape of the face. But there were anxious lines around her eyes and mouth. Her movements were hesitant, as though she were not quite sure what she ought to do.

"Oh, hi, Kate! This is Mo. My mom, I mean. Mo, this is Kate." Jessamyn was gliding down a long, curved stairway.

When Mrs. Winter excused herself to finish dinner, I turned to Jessamyn. "There's a waterfall in your living room!" I gasped.

Jessamyn laughed. "I saw it in a model home and talked Mo into buying it." We plumped down into a sofa upholstered in something nubbly and off-white.

"Jessamyn, your house is beautiful!"

Jessamyn tossed her head. "It's okay. We . . ."

The front door burst open and a fat kid stomped in, chomping down on a candy bar. A trail of mud followed him across the pristine floor as he headed for the stairs. "Mo!" Jessamyn shouted. "Courtney's doing it again!"

"Courtney?" Mrs. Winter appeared from the kitchen. "Courtney, I told you not to . . . Courtney!"

The kid completely ignored her. He bit off a huge hunk of Mr. Goodbar, pushed his thick glasses up his nose and lumbered upstairs, tracking dirt.

Mrs. Winter looked after him, helpless. Embarrassed, I stared at the tracks. Hiking boots. Wait a minute. And hadn't I seen a Mr. Goodbar wrapper on the lake bed this morning?

When Mrs. Winter went back into the kitchen, Jessamyn shook her head.

"Poor Mo. She feels sorry for him because he doesn't have a father, so she lets him walk all over her."

"He doesn't have a . . . Your father is . . ."

"He died twelve years ago, when Courtney was one."

"Oh. I'm . . . sorry," I said.

Jessamyn shrugged, picking at the nubbly things on the couch. "I hardly remember him. We're provided for and everything, so it's okay." She looked up at me. "Sometimes, I wish Mo would remarry, though."

Wow. No father. For the first time, I really felt sorry for Jessamyn.

For dinner we had asparagus tips in a sauce with a French name, plus something wrapped in puff pastry with another French name. Jessamyn said her mother was practicing on us. She had to cook for her gourmet group next week. I tried to remember those French names—you probably needed to know about things like that, living in Blue Heron—but forgot them anyway.

I hoped Courtney would let something slip about what he'd been doing to get his boots so muddy, but all he said during dinner was please pass this and please pass that. The rest of the time he chowed down, nonstop.

Mrs. Winter asked Jessamyn what she could do for the party, and Jessamyn said nothing, she'd need some money, was all. Mrs. Winter seemed to want to help. Could she decorate? Send out invitations?

"Mo, I keep telling you. You don't send out invitations. Decorations are dumb. And remember, you have to be gone by eight."

Mrs. Winter looked disappointed, but to my amazement she agreed to leave. Then she turned to me. "And what does your father do, Kate?"

Ah, Standard Question Number Two. (Number One is "And what do you want to be when you grow up?")

"He writes books." The less said, the better.

"Oh, an author!" Mrs. Winter really perked up. "What name does he use? His own or a pen name?"

"Just his own. David Hardin."

"Hmm, David Hardin." She smiled apologetically. "I'm afraid I'm not much of a reader. But my friend Carol is. Would you tell me some of the books he's written, so I can tell Carol?"

"They're really not all that well-known," I stalled.

"That's all right."

"I'm sure your friend hasn't heard of them."

"Come on, Kate," Jessamyn said. "Out with them."

"Uh, *Adventures in Gutters and Down Spouts, Everything You Always Wanted to Know about Plasterboard but Were Afraid to Ask, The Joy of Shrubs...*"

"Oh," said Mrs. Winter faintly. "Anything else?"

"Dad's written fifteen books, not counting his latest, which..." I caught myself too late.

"And what's that, dear?"

"Dollars in Your Compost Heap," I mumbled into my puff pastry.

"How nice," Mrs. Winter murmured.

"Now he's writing a book about our house," I added. "That's why it's so beat-up. I mean, he had to buy a house with, um, deferred maintenance items so he could fix it up for his book. Otherwise we would have, you know, bought a newer house or..." I trailed off lamely.

"Of course, dear," Mrs. Winter said. "More asparagus?"

After dinner, we went up to Jessamyn's room. We sat on her white lace coverlet and talked about boys—Jessamyn's boyfriend was a sophomore at Portland State—and clothes. Jessamyn pulled a spiral notebook from a drawer and handed it to me. It was filled with fashion drawings, the sketchy kind like you sometimes see in the newspapers. Some of the clothes were really wild. Others looked more normal, but with unusual little touches.

"Wow, Jessamyn, did you do these?"

"Uh-huh."

"They're fantastic! Have you ever actually made up any of them?"

"You mean like sewed them?" Jessamyn wrinkled her nose. "I don't sew. I'm into name labels. Only someday I want the name on the labels to be mine!" Jessamyn showed me the new shirt she'd bought for her party. The name on the label sounded familiar. Underneath, I read, "100 percent silk." The shirt was lavender, with buttoned flaps on the front pockets and cute little epaulettes on the shoulders. "Everybody wears pants to parties,'' she explained, ''so the shirt you wear is very important. Our school is N.F.O.''

''N.F.O.?''

''Natural Fibers Only. Silk, linen, cotton, wool. Polyester is out.''

''Oh.'' I swallowed. Practically everything I owned was polyester, or at least had polyester in it. Mom's the world's most ardent polyester fan. To her, polyester is a Miracle of Modern Chemistry rivaled only by fortified dry cereal and Naugahyde. ''You can wash it in the machine, you don't have to iron it, it looks fine and it actually costs less than materials you have to dry clean,'' she says. ''Why people buy anything else, I'll never understand.''

''The outfit you have on now is very sweet,'' Jessamyn was saying, ''and I'm sure it's just right for Colorado, but—I hope you don't mind my giving you some advice...''

''Oh, no, please do!''

''Hey, I know. Mo and I are going shopping tomorrow. If you like, I could help you pick out some clothes like the ones kids are wearing here. Want to come?''

''Oh, yes!''

Actually, I thought, walking home, I wasn't sure I'd be able to go. Mom would probably expect me to help clean and put things away. But I'd never asked to move here. I had to leave all my friends and start over and I had a right not to be the laughingstock of Blue Heron, didn't I? I kicked hard at a rock at the side of the road, heard it skitter away into the darkness. The thing was...I stopped. *What was that?* I could swear I saw a light flicker through the trees near the side of the road. Slowly, I swung my flashlight in a wide arc. Black shadows spiked away from me, then massed together as the beam moved away. "Who's there?" I called.

My heart pounded in my ears. Beyond that, silence.

"Hello?"

No answer. I raked over the woods with my flashlight one more time. No sign of anything weird, any light other than my own. I am a basket case, a real basket case, I muttered to myself.

I ran the rest of the way home.

The front door yielded to a firm bump of the hip, a technique I'd perfected while helping the movers.

"Kate? How'd it go?" Mom called from the kitchen. She and Dad sat tranquilly in a sea of plastic pellets, crumpled paper and cardboard boxes.

"Oh, fine." I stood there a minute, catching my breath. "You wouldn't believe their house. It has a waterfall in the living room."

"Probably an economy measure," said Dad. "I bet they stock it with salmon and catch one for dinner every night."

"Very funny, Dad." I hesitated, searching for the best way to approach the shopping subject.

"You know the party Jessamyn's having Friday night?"

"Yes, wasn't that nice of her to invite you," said Mom.

"Uh-huh. The thing is, I need a new blouse. And Jessamyn and her mother are going shopping tomorrow and they've invited me to go along. Jessamyn's going to help me pick out the kind of things kids here wear to parties and . . ."

"Whoa there! Hold on!" Dad broke in. "I thought you spent all your baby-sitting money on those videos you gave Becky when we left."

"Well, I did, but . . ."

"What's wrong with the blouses you have?" asked Mom. "Your burgundy print is very nice."

"But Mom, that's not the kind of thing kids in Blue Heron wear. Jessamyn told me."

"Besides, I need you to help me tomorrow. We've got a lot of unpacking to do, and I start at the lab on Monday." Mom stood and began stuffing paper and pellets into a plastic trash bag. "I'm sorry, Kate. Ordinarily I'd help you sew something for the party, but we just don't have time right now."

"Sew something! Don't you understand? Blue Heron kids don't make their own clothes! They buy them, and only certain brands. It's all right for you guys to go around wearing any old thing. You don't care, anyway. But I'm not going to ruin the next three years of my life just because you don't care if I ever have friends again or not! I didn't ask to move here anyway. You brought me into this rich neighborhood and now I'm stuck living in it."

Dad and Mom stared at me, speechless. "Katie . . ." Dad started to say at last, but I couldn't answer. I had to go shopping tomorrow. I refused to be a social pariah for the rest of my high school years! I fled from the room and stomped upstairs.

Chapter Five

If you've ever stomped upstairs in a huff, you'll remember that the dramatic effect wears off entirely too soon. In short, you feel ridiculous. So I cut out the stomping and walked normally down the hall and up to the turret room.

It was quiet up here. Shadows webbed over the edges of the room. I picked up my photo album and sat in the middle of the floor, in the small bright patch cast by the bare bulb overhead.

There was the sad-faced boy in the sailor suit. There was the man in white. There was Elise. Still beautiful, still charming the socks off everyone. I tried to imagine Elise as a gangly fifteen-year-old with adjustment problems. Impossible. Maybe she'd been one of those people who just up and blooms one day. Like Becky, in Colorado. She'd looked in the mirror, and miracle of miracles ...

I flung open the trunk and found it, the white velvet cape. I draped it over my shoulders, twisted my hair back and up off my neck, then sat up straight in front of the mirror. Chin up, shoulders back. There.

All at once the feeling was there again. The magical feeling. The girl in the mirror smiled, a slow, confident, meltingly beautiful smile. Something about this room released her—my secret, other self. Not the self whose clothes flunked the N.F.O. test. Whose tongue turned to wood whenever there was a good-looking guy around. No. If the girl in the mirror went to the party Friday night, heads would turn and voices would buzz: "Who is that?" The guys would crowd around; she would laugh and know exactly what to say.

"Elise, show me how," I whispered. I snatched up the album from the floor and stared hard at Elise, as though I could ferret out her secret if only....

A soft yellow glow, like sunrise, spread over the mirror. Behind my right shoulder I saw reflected a hand, disembodied, hanging in the air. I twisted around and it was still there, just beyond the window. It hovered for an endless moment, then one finger separated itself out from the rest and began to trace something in the dirt on the glass.

ITS, it wrote.

The scream stuck way back in my throat. I tried to force it out, but it wouldn't budge, not even a piece of it, not even a whisper.

MINE, it wrote.

The hand disappeared and my scream ripped loose, filled the room. Far away, beyond the scream, I heard a shattering sound. Then I was at the window and a dark shape crawled down through the air, and a blaze of light flared up from the ground, and then Dad and Mom were looking out with me and I realized the screaming had stopped.

"You two stay here." Dad plunged down the stairs, two at a time. Mom and I looked at each other, then we were running downstairs after him. Amy stumbled into the hallway, rubbing her eyes.

"Stay here, Ames," I said. I ran through the hall, down the stairs, out the front door. Behind me I heard the thump thump of Amy's bare feet and Cyrano's unmistakable snortings and gruntings.

Mom and Dad were already there when I got to the base of the turret. Raindrops danced in the flashlight beam as Dad traced the long lines of a ladder propped against the turret and reaching to a couple of yards below its top windows.

"Darn," Dad said. His light lingered at the top of the ladder, then flicked to the ground, skittered around and zeroed in on a lantern's dented metal frame. Shards of yellow glass glittered in the rain.

"I guess we're going to have to call the police after all." Mom's voice was quiet.

"I guess so." Dad ran his hand through his damp hair. "I'd hoped it wouldn't come to this. I really didn't think it would."

"I know you didn't." Mom put her hand on his arm.

I felt as though I'd come in in the middle of a scary movie, and everyone knew whodunnit but me. "What's going on? What do you two know you're not telling?"

Mom sighed. "Come in the house, Kate. It's about time you ... Good grief, Amy. Just look at you!"

Amy's nightgown, half pink, half muck, had torn loose from its ruffle, which tangled around her feet. "Cyrano tripped me."

"Into the house, all of you!" Mom ordered.

Half an hour later, everyone who needed scrubbing had been scrubbed and everyone who needed drying had been dried. Amy had been changed, storied and tucked in for the second time that night. Mom, Dad and I sat at the kitchen table with steaming cups of freeze-dried coffee and instant cocoa. Dad explained how a woman who lived across the lake, a Miss Watts or somebody, had seen a light inside this house several times over the last month. The woman had told the real estate agent about it, but nobody, apparently, had called the police.

"So you don't know who it was," I said.

"No. But for years there's been a rumor about a treasure around here somewhere," Dad said. "We figured the snooping would end once we moved in."

"Is that how the bit about the ghost with the yellow lantern got started? Treasure hunters?"

"How did you know about the yellow lantern?"

"Everybody knows about it. Jessamyn told me the whole story."

"Oh. Well, that's the odd part," Dad continued. "This ghost story or whatever you want to call it, has been going around since Elise Mathieson disappeared, back in '28. But now a lantern really turns up. It's screwy. That's why I got mad when you didn't tell us about the light last night. I guess I should have told you about all this, but we didn't want to upset you kids."

"It's not as though Amy and I are the same, you know," I protested. "I'm fifteen, and she's only four."

"I know, I know. Your mom and I are going to have to be more aware of that."

I smiled weakly, but my mind was whirring backward, freeze-framing on scenes from the last couple of days. Kirk's theory about the kids. Jessamyn saying the neighborhood kids hadn't wanted us to move in here, "especially my brother." Courtney's muddy hiking boots and the Mr. Goodbar.

Mom suddenly pushed her chair back. "Oh, dear. The police. I almost forgot. I'll run over to the O'Briens' and call."

"Mom." I jumped up. "Mom, please don't call the police."

She stared at me. "What?"

"Please don't. I think I...I may know who did it." I told Mom and Dad how Kirk and I had found the footprints. They already knew about the lake being drained, another detail they'd neglected to mention. Then I told them the stuff about Courtney.

"This is all very interesting, Kate, but it's far from conclusive," Mom said. "How would a thirteen-year-old get that ladder all the way over here? It's huge. And the lantern..."

"He's a big kid. Or maybe he had help, I don't know. Anyway, he didn't actually do anything."

"Didn't do anything! He invaded our property and scared the living daylights out of us. And who knows what would have happened if that ladder had reached all the way up to the windows."

"Mom, please! If you call the police, and I have to tell them about Courtney—or even if I don't but they figure out he did it—how will I ever stay friends with Jessamyn? My life is messed up enough already without you guys siccing the police on my only friend's brother. Her mom would hate me forever."

Dad ran his hand through his hair. "It does have the look of a childish prank, Jeanne. I mean, going to all that trouble to write 'It's mine' in the dirt on a window? Pretty juvenile stuff."

"What if it isn't Courtney? And what if this keeps up? We can't go on living like this." Mom shook her head. She walked back to the table and sat down. "Kate. I realize it's got to be tough for you, starting all over here. Your dad and I have been talking, and we've decided it will be all right for you to go shopping tomorrow with Jessamyn and her mother. But I don't see how we can..."

"If it happens one more time, we'll call the police. Okay, Mom? Please?"

Mom hesitated. "All right. But just one more time, and..."

"Thanks, Mom!" I hugged her, closing my eyes, hoping I was right to fear Jessamyn's mom more than the dark shape that crawled down into the night.

"We're going to Nordie's. Nordstrom's, downtown Portland," Jessamyn said, turning to face me from the front seat of her mother's copper-colored Mercedes the next day. I sat in back; the smells of leather and wood polish mingled in my nose.

"And Mo's taking us out to lunch. She's buying us cocktails, too." Jessamyn winked at me and arched an eyebrow at her mother, in the driver's seat.

"I'm what?" Mrs. Winter sounded startled. "Oh," she said. "You're kidding."

She dropped us at Nordstrom's front door and drove off to park the car. We were supposed to meet her at noon.

We glided up the escalator to the third floor, past a gigantic mirrored wall. Sportswear. Jessamyn wove effortlessly through the maze of racks, homing in on the designer section as if by remote control. She picked out a shirt, some slacks and a blazer, and paid for them with a credit card.

Next we went to the shoe salon, where Jessamyn got a pair of short Italian boots, which she wore. And on to fine jewelry, where she charged a long, twisted gold chain. I gasped when I saw how much it cost. Jessamyn laughed. "Mo won't mind," she said. "She wants me to have all the things she couldn't afford when she was my age."

Then it was back downstairs, where Jessamyn picked out an elegant angora-and-silk sweater.

Meanwhile, I felt a bad case of the "wanties" coming on. I can go for months without buying much if I stay out of the stores. But plunk me down in the middle of a place like this and suddenly I discover a thousand things I can't possibly live without. Like the emerald-green silk blouse I'd just pulled off the sale rack.

"That would look super on you, Katharyn!" said Jessamyn.

"Oh, I don't think so," I said, trying not to be too obvious about my frantic search for the price tag.

"Yes, it's perfect. Let's see." She held it up near my face. "The color is great on you."

"Oh, thanks, but I don't really think so." I'd found the tag. Bad news.

"Try it on. You'll see I'm right."

"No, I really..."

"Come on." Jessamyn gripped my elbow and practically manhandled me into a dressing room. "There," she said a few moments later. "I knew it. It's gorgeous. I just love dolman sleeves, don't you?"

I stood looking in the mirror. The blouse felt slippery on my skin. It shimmered slightly. And the color did do something for me, I had to admit. The wanties came on like a mean flu virus.

"This is just the thing for my party," Jessamyn was saying. "You'll be a hit! With a little gold chain, oh, about so long..."

"A gold ch..." I choked.

"I've got one I hardly ever wear. You can borrow it."

Sixty-two dollars. For just one blouse. On sale. And you couldn't even wash it yourself, not even by hand. Mom would flip.

"I'll think about it," I said.

"You don't have time to think about it. The party's tomorrow night."

"But I don't have any money with me."

"No problem. I'll charge it. You can pay us back later. And if you decide you don't like it, you'd be nuts but no problem. Nordie's lets you return it, no questions asked."

"But my mom might say no."

"Oh, come on, Katharyn." Now Jessamyn sounded really exasperated. "How can she refuse? It's an investment. Tell you what. I'll drop by your house when we take you home and help you convince her. I can be very persuasive."

"Well..." Mom hadn't actually said I couldn't buy anything. Maybe if I baby-sat to pay it off... "Well, all right."

But my money problems had just begun, as I found out at lunch.

"Katharyn, you've just got to sign up for the Saturday ski trips," Jessamyn said, pushing aside the last of her quiche.

"It's only two hundred dollars for every Saturday in February," added Mrs. Winter. "Very reasonable, don't you think?"

I nodded and swallowed hard. "Oh, yes. Very." How could I explain that I hadn't even figured out how to scrounge sixty-two dollars for the blouse I was taking home today, much less two hundred dollars for skiing? I didn't need my calculator to figure that, at my rate for baby-sitting Amy, I'd have to put in two hundred hours to go skiing. Compared to what Jessamyn and her mother had spent today, two hundred dollars seemed like such a puny, pathetic amount. But right now I was as far from having two hundred dollars as from...driving a Mercedes.

All during the ride home I mentally rehearsed what I would say to Mom to convince her to buy me that blouse. I'd be up against a confirmed polyester fanatic. But Jessamyn was very persuasive. Together, we might bring it off.

I hadn't counted on the sudden disaster which struck as I opened the front door.

I used the hip-bump technique I'd perfected earlier. The door swung part way open, then stopped with a crack. There was a clattering crash, a shout, then the thud of a body hitting the floor.

Chapter Six

Cyrano, covered with whitish glop, squirted through the door, slammed into Jessamyn's new Italian boots and streaked across the front yard.

Jessamyn stared at the goo on her boots. "What is it?"

"Katie?" came Dad's voice from inside. "That you?" There was a scraping noise; the door opened wider, and Dad stepped out. He had a bloody cut on his forehead.

"Dad! Are you okay?" I asked.

"What is it?" Jessamyn said.

"I'm fine. That's, uh, wallpaper paste, Jessie. It'll come right off with warm water and soap—I think. I was up a ladder with a bucket of the stuff when the door knocked into me, and Cyrano..."

"Wallpaper paste! Oh no! My boots are ruined!" Jessamyn turned on her heel and half walked, half jogged toward her house.

"Bye, Jessamyn," I called after her.

Dad and I silently watched her leave. Dad sighed. "I guess Jessie's not used to home remodeling."

"I guess not."

"She seems pretty upset about her boots."

"She just bought them. They're Italian."

"Oh." Dad ran his hand through his hair, leaving a trail of white paste globules. "I'm sorry, Katie. We must seem a little strange to some of the people around here. But when they get to know us better..."

Funny thing. Most of the time I can tough it out. Give me a little sympathy, though, and it's all over. Tears welled up and trickled down my cheeks. Dad drew a spattered rag through his belt loop and handed it to me.

"It's just... it's just so *hard*!"

"I know it, honey."

"I'll never have any friends." I sniffed and pawed through the rag, searching for a clean spot.

"Yes you will. You're a very likeable person. You'll..."

"Oh, you don't understand." I blew my nose and thrust the rag at Dad. "I'm sorry, Dad. And I didn't mean to knock you over. It's just..."

"I know."

No you don't, I thought. You have no idea.

After changing into my grubbies, I set off across the hillside to find Cyrano. I had a hunch he'd be off chasing ducks in the bay.

A murky fog formed droplets on my face and hair. It blurred out the sky, so I couldn't tell for certain whether the sun had set or not. Only five o'clock, and Dad had made me take the flashlight, it was so dark.

"Cyrano!" I called. The Bay of Footprints gradually took shape out of the grayness ahead. Closer, I could see that the footprints were practically all washed out. Rain, no doubt. Where they'd been, a tangle of fresh paw prints ran across the mud. Paw prints, and a mess of other prints.

Duck prints.

"Cyrano! Come on, boy! Cyrano!" Silence pressed in around me as I stood at the edge of the lake bed. A heaviness settled over me like a thick wool blanket. A damp heaviness of air, the whole heavy hopelessness of my day with Jessamyn. A heavy dread of water, water rising in the lake.

"Cyrano, would you get over here, you dumb mutt!"

Not a chance. I took a deep breath, sat on the bank, then stepped in.

Mud sucked at my shoes. I concentrated hard on the prints. There. A line of paw prints branched off from the tangle and disappeared in the fog. They headed toward our house, along the inside edge of the lake bed. I picked my way between puddles and tree stumps, beneath a diving board on stilts above the mud.

Now the cliff which formed the lake basin rose sharply beside me. I was out of the bay now, in the main lake near our house. Yesterday there'd been water here; today it was empty except for a small pond in the middle.

"Cyrano!" An answering snort, the squishy pad pad of little paws. "There you are!" Cyrano, mud-caked, appeared out of the fog. I could hear the vanquished ducks quacking in the distance. "You are disgusting!" Cyrano wagged all over, snorting so furiously I was afraid he was headed for another attack.

"Did you figure out a muddier way home, boy?" Maybe we could get back this way, if we could find those steps we saw yesterday, the ones leading into the lake.

Yes. There they were. But now not only were the steps out of water, the bottom one was five feet up. It curved out in a semicircle well beyond the others; more like a platform than a step. A concrete wall rose from the lake bed to support the platform and steps.

"Up you go, Cyrano." I lifted him to the platform, shutting my eyes against a spray of mud and loose dirt. Then I put my hands on the platform, jumped and scrambled up. Home free.

I stood a minute, catching my breath. What a strange setup! A bunch of steps leading into a lake. For swimmers, maybe? But the platform and all of the steps would normally be under water. And another odd thing. Both ends of the platform butted up against the rock cliff face. Which was okay, except that, where one end of the platform met the cliff, there was this patch of brickwork. In the middle of the rock. A couple bricks looked about to fall out, so I tugged on one. It came loose and chunked onto the lake bed. It looked hollow behind the brick. I put both hands into the hole and pulled. A shower of bricks and cement chunks tumbled onto the lake bed as I stared, unbelieving.

Into a cave.

Standing there, looking at that cave, a whole lot of thoughts started churning around in my head. Thoughts about Elise and how she'd disappeared. About silk blouses and ski trips.

About hidden treasure.

My breath came faster. My heart thudded in my chest.

I cleared out a few more bricks, pulled the flashlight from my pocket and crawled through the hole.

It was dark in there and fairly dry except for a few puddles on the floor. Slowly, I stood, expecting my head to bump at any moment; it didn't. Swinging the flashlight beam around, I saw I was at the mouth of a kind of tunnel. Something rubbed against my leg; I jumped and flashed the light down. "Cyrano! You scared me, boy." I took a deep breath. "Okay, let's check this out."

The cave floor, level at first, began to slant up as we walked, becoming steeper and steeper until it formed rough steps. I counted eleven of them, and then they ended.

I flicked my light around. We were in a cavern. Or maybe not a cavern, exactly, but a widening in the passageway, to a room about the size of Jessamyn's walk-in closet. Stacked in the center of the floor was a whole bunch of wooden crates. They looked sort of like the wine crates you see in some delicatessens, except these were really rotten. In places the wood had disintegrated, and I could see something—I shone my light over them—it looked like wine bottles inside.

My flashlight beam glanced over the walls, the floor, the ceiling. Nothing but the crates and bottles and a pile of boulders and rocky debris near one wall.

Then that was it. A wine cellar. How boring. I leaned against a boulder, feeling hope crumble within me like decayed wood.

Except... idly I played the light around the cave. Except it didn't make sense. The whole bottom part of the cave—including the entrance—would be under water most of the time. And bricked over. Why would anybody...

Something glinted, half-sunk in a collapsed crate. A small, rusty metal box. Carefully, I lifted it out. It was heavy. Something shifted inside. I squatted on the floor, dug my fingernails under the lid and pried hard. The lid popped loose, shedding great flakes of rust.

Coins. Old coins.

I picked up one. A fifty-cent piece. It had some lady in a diaphanous gown with her arm reaching out toward the sunrise or sunset, I couldn't tell which. It felt hard and cold and heavy in my hand.

I dropped it into the box and dug through the coins. Silver dollars and half dollars. I poured them into my lap and clanked them one by one back into the box. Sixty-one silver dollars, thirty half dollars. No jewelry or anything else.

Seventy-six dollars. I sighed. If this was the treasure, it was way overrated. Cyrano waddled over and sniffed hopefully at the box.

"Nothing to eat, boy. Just money."

Still, it had to be worth more than seventy-six dollars. Just how much more, I wasn't sure. But they were old, I could tell. I dug out a handful and checked the date on each coin. 1928 was the most recent one there.

Okay, so now what? I take the coins and give them to Mom and Dad. They give them to the police. Then we wait until someone claims them. How long? I once found five dollars on the playground and it took months before they decided it didn't belong to anybody and I could have it.

On the other hand, if I took the coins now and sold them...

"You should give them to your parents," went this little voice inside my head.

It's too little to help them, and anyway I'm just saying what if. I could sell the coins and get the money. It would be enough to pay for my blouse. Maybe the ski trips, too. And then...then I could buy them back, later. With the baby-sitting money I'm going to earn.

"They aren't yours," said the voice.

True, but whose were they?

I shivered as an eerie idea struck. Elise. What if they had been hers? What if she were watching over me, taking care of me, putting these coins in my way just when I needed them most?

That's ridiculous.

I raked my fingers through the coins, thinking. Now that the cave was open, anyone could come in and find them. Courtney or another one of the neighbor kids, or...suddenly I remembered the message on the window: It's mine.

I decided to take them to my room. Just for safe-keeping. Later, I could figure out what to do.

"Come on, boy. Let's go home."

That night after dinner I showed Mom and Dad the blouse. "100 percent silk," Mom read from the label. "Don't they make anything in polyester? I get so mad at these manufacturers. Why do they make things you can't wash when we have perfectly fine synthetics available?''

"No one at Blue Heron High wears polyester. They're N.F.O."

"What in the world is N.F.O.?"

"Natural Fibers Only. You know. Silk, cotton, linen, wool. Polyester's out."

"Now that's not very logical, do you think?"

"Mom! I don't make the rules, I just . . ."

"Follow?" Mom looked at me for a minute. "Kate, I've never thought of you as a follower. You've always done your own thinking. And we've been so proud of you for that."

"Look, you said you'd try to help me out on this. You didn't say you were going to dictate what I wear. Now are you going to help me or are you going back on your promise?"

"Katie, there's something you should know." Dad glanced quickly at Mom before going on. "I gave up my advance."

"What? What do you mean?"

"My editor moved to another publishing house, and I heard through the grapevine that my new editor wasn't committed to the book. She'll publish it, sure, but she won't promote it. That's like condemning it to a quick death. Thing is, I really believe in this book. I know it'll sell like hot cakes given half a chance." Dad grinned. "Of course we'll all be rich and famous in the end, you know that." I didn't. "So anyway, I gave back the advance and withdrew the book."

"So what does that mean?"

"It means we're on a bare-bones budget for a while. Just until I find another publisher, which should be—well, pretty soon."

"How soon is pretty soon?"

"Could be a couple of weeks, or maybe longer. Listen, Katie. Things'll go on pretty much as before. We'll eat, you don't have to worry about that. You may have to baby-sit Amy more than usual; Mom's going to be the sole breadwinner for a while. But we'll keep track of your hours and pay you when the new advance comes through. Other than that, we'll just be cutting the frills—vacations, potato chips, phones, fancy new clothes... Just until the, uh, temporary cash flow problem eases up."

"Did you say phones?"

"Only until the new advance comes in."

"And what if another publisher doesn't take it? Then we're stuck here, in this—this house, in a neighborhood where if you're not practically a millionaire you're some kind of a weirdo."

"Kate, hush," Mom said. "We're sorry this had to happen but that's the way it is. We'll expect everyone to pull together and help out."

"After all," Dad said cheerfully, "money isn't everything."

"Oh, right." I stared down at the table. "I look bad enough to begin with, but without decent clothes..."

"Nonsense, you're a very pretty girl," Mom said.

"You have a lot of potential," Dad added.

"Oh, please!"

I walked out of the room and upstairs to the turret room, fighting to keep cool. I felt bad for Dad about the book. I felt bad about acting so crummy. But my own problems were just so horrible.

Now I had no choice. I had to use those coins.

Anyway I was just borrowing them. It wouldn't be any different than what Mom and Dad were doing about my baby-sitting money. I'd keep track and pay it all back later. I had a temporary cash flow problem, that's all.

Besides, it wasn't even anybody's money anyway. I found it, didn't I? Who would ever know? Who would it hurt?

No one. It was no big deal.

Chapter Seven

The problem with a life of crime is you do one thing wrong, then you have to go around lying practically forever to cover up.

"Hey, Mom, I'd like to check out Blue Heron a bit. Just to get to know the town."

Lie Number One. What I really planned to do was find a place to sell my coins. Trouble was, we had no phone book. Heck, we had no phone. So I'd have to find it on foot.

"Amy can come, too," I said. "I'll even buy her some ice cream."

Mom looked at me strangely. "I thought you were low on funds."

"I am, but I think I can swing a couple of ice-cream cones."

"Okay. But be back by one."

Amy and I walked to a gas station phone booth I'd noticed in town. In the yellow pages, under "Coin Dealers, Supplies, Etc." I found it. Blue Heron Coin and Stamp. I wrote down the address, then asked the gas station attendant for directions. Six blocks away. Not bad.

At the shop I dug the coins from my purse and spread them out on the counter. The man bent over and studied them, one at a time, his thick black brows contracting.

"Where did you get these?" he demanded, at last.

"I...it's a collection. I've been...collecting...for a long time."

Lie Number Two.

The man squinted at me, saying nothing.

"Where's the ice cream?" Amy asked.

"This isn't the ice-cream store. We're going there next."

"What store is this? What is that money for?"

"Nothing. Hey, why don't you look out the door and see if you can spot the ice-cream store? It's across the street."

Amy trotted to the doorway.

"I only want to sell about sixty-five dollars worth," I said.

"Do your parents know you're doing this?"

"Yes. Well, no, actually. It's...sort of a surprise." My face felt hot. I wondered if the coin man reported suspicious characters—like me—to the police.

He was squinting at me again. Finally he separated out three coins. "I can pay you seventy for these. They're pretty rare. Or two fifty for the works."

"Just these, please," I said, pointing to the three.

"Are you sure?" The man fondled a coin between his fingers. "I could go, maybe, two seventy-five."

"No. Just the three."

I had a creepy feeling about the guy. Something about the way he looked at me. I couldn't tell if he were so honest he might report me to the police, or so dishonest he might get those coins by whatever means he could.

"Smile, Katharyn! You're gonna be gorgeous!"

I managed a weak grin, but at this point I doubted it. Jessamyn had scrubbed my face with some sort of sandpapery stuff and put my hair in hot rollers. I looked awful. On her bathroom counter sprawled an arsenal of bottles, jars, tubes, powders, brushes and swabs.

"I know I need help, but this is ridiculous."

"Oh, relax. When I'm done you'll look like you're hardly wearing any makeup at all."

"You're kidding."

"Nope. Now shut up, please. We don't have much time, and I can't concentrate while you're blabbing."

Jessamyn spun my chair so that I faced away from the mirror. She swabbed my face with something cool and tingly. Funny. In some ways she reminded me of Dad. Both utterly confident about beautifying a hopeless wreck.

But thinking of Dad stirred up a flurry of unsettling memories. Because the lies hadn't ended that morning. Later, after Jessamyn had invited me to come early and spend the night when the party was over, I'd had to figure out how to con Mom and Dad into thinking I wasn't wearing the silk blouse at the party. So I put an old blouse in the Nordstrom's bag and left it on my bed. I packed the silk one in my overnight case. It wasn't a lie, not really. But an uneasy feeling came over me every time I closed my eyes and saw that dumb bag on the bed.

Then, when I'd paid Mrs. Winter for the blouse, I told her my parents had paid for it. Lie Number Four.

"Voila!" Jessamyn put down my hairbrush. "Now go get dressed, and don't you dare look in the mirror until you're done. I want to see the expression on your face."

I did as I was told, then returned to the bathroom mirror. "Wow," I breathed. I looked great. For me, I mean. All the little bumps and splotches had vanished from my face. My eyes looked big; my hair fluffed out around my face; my blouse shimmered. I still looked like me, only different, like the person I saw in the mirror in the turret room at night.

"Wow," I said again.

So that's what it takes to be beautiful. A silk blouse. A gold chain. A whole bunch of jars and tubes and brushes.

"You're welcome," said Jessamyn. "All in a day's work for an artistic genius. Wish I had time to do you in my sketchbook, but the kids'll be here any minute." She tossed her head and examined herself critically in the mirror as her hair flared out in its silky fan. "Actually, I may have overdone it. You'll be the hit of my party."

She laughed a laugh that told me I was no threat. Still, I knew it was going to be a magical New Year's Eve. I could feel it. I could just feel it.

When the first kids arrived, Jessamyn introduced me around. They were real nice, not snobbish or anything like that.

After a while they bunched into groups, talking about stuff I didn't know about, people I didn't know. I sort of hovered around, listening, smiling, nodding, groping for some way to break in. Someone said something about the rain, and I saw my chance. "My dad says Oregonians don't tan," I heard myself say, "they rust."

For a long moment, everybody looked at me. All of a sudden my face felt hot. This one girl smiled politely, and then they were all talking again, and I was smiling again and telling myself, what did you expect, anyway? To be Miss Popularity? My hands felt awkward, as if they'd forgotten what hands are supposed to do.

Pretty soon the lights got turned down and the music got turned up. The room filled so full of kids I could hardly move. How could anyone tell I was wearing a real silk blouse and a real gold chain?

I squeezed through the crowd, searching for faces, the face of someone I knew, maybe, or the face of someone else who had no one to talk to. Jessamyn had disappeared with her college boyfriend, Nick, ages ago. A bunch of people were milling around the back door, drinking from plastic cups. A tall, good-looking guy stood just inside the door. He winked at me, so I smiled back, feeling for the first time in hours that this party might turn out okay after all. He draped his arms around me and breathed a beery "Hey, baby," into my face. Then he was leaning on me, crushing me with his weight, pawing at me with his hands. I twisted away and shoved through the crowd.

My head throbbed from the loud music. My whole face ached from smiling so long, pretending I was having fun. I hate this party, I thought. I don't care about Jessamyn, I'm getting my bag, I'm going home. Blindly I shoved through the bodies toward the stairs.

"Hey, Kate, where you going?"

I was so amazed to hear my name, I couldn't answer.

"Kate! Over here!"

It was Kirk. With his freckles and his jug ears and his old army jacket, he was a far cry from the dark, rugged stranger I'd had in mind. Still, when I recognized him, a nice feeling washed over me. Relief, I think it was.

"Hi," I said.

"I've been trying to gd odda thiziz du bidblus," he said. Or sounds to that effect.

"What?"

"I said . . ." More incoherent sounds, drowned out by loud music, loud talk and loud laughter.

"I can't hear you!"

"I'm going outside!" he yelled into my ear and set off through the crowd. Then, as an afterthought, he shouted, "You can come if you want."

Ah, romance.

Outside, the air felt fresh and cool. I drank in a breath. It smelled of pine.

"Any new developments in the Mystery of the Underwater Ghost?" asked Kirk, flopping down on the front steps.

"Give me a break, would you." I sat down next to him.

"Okay. Seriously, anything?"

I told him what had happened with the window Wednesday night.

"Wow. Did you call the cops?"

"No." I shrugged. "I hate to admit it, but you could be right about the kids possibility. Besides..."

"Besides what?"

"Listen, don't tell anybody I said this, okay?"

Kirk shrugged. "Okay."

"Jessamyn's brother's hiking boots were really muddy when I came over here Wednesday for dinner. Plus he was eating a Mr. Goodbar. Did you see that Mr. Goodbar wrapper in the lake?"

Kirk shook his head.

"Well, I saw one. It still doesn't prove anything, though, but..."

"So it was Courtney?"

"Well, I don't know for sure. But it's a..."

"I know, a possibility." I made a face. Kirk grinned. "To you it's a possibility. To me it's about certain."

"Hey, I still say there's lots of possibilities." I ticked them off on my fingers. "The kids possibility, the treasure-hunter possibility, the haunting possibility..."

"Huh!" Kirk snorted.

"And the robber possibility, and lots of other possibilities we haven't even thought of."

"Why would a robber write on your window? It doesn't make sense. And why would he pick your house? It isn't exactly the ritziest target on the lake."

I felt the blood rush to my face. "You think I don't know that?"

Kirk leveled his light gray eyes at me. "I didn't realize you were sensitive about it," he said, finally.

I couldn't think of anything to say. I guess Kirk couldn't either, because he sat silent for a few minutes. Raindrops tapped at the roof over our heads; music throbbed behind us. I shivered, rubbed my arms, and soon I was talking, telling Kirk about Elise and her clothes and the scrapbook, and before I knew it I was telling him about the cave and the wine bottles, everything except the money. I couldn't tell him about that. He listened until I was through and then asked, "Did you get a look at the dates on the wine labels by any chance?"

"Why? Do you—hey, you want to drink it! You want to know if it was any good!"

"Oh, jeez, Kate! How dumb can you be! Do you know what was happening in 1928?"

"I just told you, that's when Elise disappeared."

"I know that. But what was going on nationally in 1928?"

"Uh, the Depression?"

Kirk sighed and shook his head. "Prohibition, dummy. Don't you get it? If that wine was put into the cave in 1928, it was illegal. Bootleg!" Kirk jumped up and started pacing around the steps.

Wow, Prohibition. I remembered reading about that. They outlawed liquor in this country for several years back then. For everybody, not just kids. So people started making it and importing it and doing all kinds of crazy stuff. Bootleg—that was the name they had for illegal liquor.

"What about this Elise woman?" Kirk demanded, still pacing. "Maybe she was bootlegging. Maybe she put it there."

"No way." I hugged my knees to my chest. "She wasn't the type."

"How do you know?"

"I just—know. She had too much class."

"You just know. That's great. And you're supposed to be the skeptic. Kate, could I..." Kirk sat down beside me. "Boy, I'd love to see that cave. Would you show it to me? We could check out the dates on the wine labels. Find out when it was put there."

"Uh, okay," I said. "But..."

Something rustled in the tall bushes on one side of the steps.

Kirk and I stared at each other. We turned and peered into the bushes. Beyond the outer leaves, which shone yellow-green in the porch light, it was black, pitch black.

"Who's there?" Kirk said.

The bushes rustled again. A chill arced up my spine and tingled at the roots of my hair.

Kirk tiptoed down the stairs. "Stay there," he whispered. Naturally, I followed.

"Who's there?" Kirk called again.

No answer.

He plunged into the bushes, and they came to life, twitching and flailing and spewing up dead leaves. Strange noises issued from inside: grunts, quackings, an "Ouch! It bit me!" Then a dark shape rose up and over my head with a beating of wings.

A duck.

Kirk emerged from the bushes pushing Courtney. "You ruined it," Courtney whined. "I planned this for weeks. And now you ruined it."

"What were you going to do with that duck?" Kirk demanded.

"Nothing."

"Don't give me that. What!" Kirk grabbed Courtney by the shoulders and shook.

"Let it loose in Jessamyn's dumb party."

Kirk looked at me. His mouth twitched. "Is that why you've been hanging around on the lake bed?"

"Yeah." Courtney pushed his glasses up his nose. "I trapped that duck. I fed it every day. It would've been great."

I pressed my lips together to keep from smiling. "Okay, so why did you write on Kate's window?" Kirk asked sternly.

"What?" Courtney looked genuinely puzzled.

"On Kate's window. What did you do that for?"

"I didn't do anything to Kate's window. Honest. I never went near there." Slowly, Kirk dropped his hands from Courtney's shoulders. Courtney clomped up the stairs and into the house. "It would've been great," he muttered. "It would've been great."

The door shut. "It would've been great," Kirk mimicked. He turned to me. "And you know something? It really would have."

"I know." I giggled.

Then Kirk giggled. We both got to giggling so hard we had to hold on to each other to keep from falling.

The door swung open again; music swelled up and engulfed us. Jessamyn sauntered unsteadily onto the porch.

"Kirk and Kate. How sweet. Are you two having fun out here?"

"I have to go now." Kirk stopped laughing abruptly and walked down the driveway.

"Your mommy calling?" Jessamyn warbled. She leaned down close to me. She smelled like beer. "I wouldn't have anything to do with him if I were you. Your basic grind type. Bo-oring."

She sniggered once, hiccupped twice and sashayed into the house.

Chapter Eight

As a result of what happened later that night, I got the worst reputation a girl in my position can have. I became known as a Good Influence.

"Oh, Katharyn, Mo just adores you," Jessamyn said the next Monday, my first day of school, as we picked at our Salisbury steak with parsleyed potatoes during lunch. "It's positively nauseating."

"It's not so bad when you cut out the gristle," I said.

"Not this thing! Mo! She keeps harping on your model behavior Friday night. 'Katharyn was in control of herself,' she says. 'Imagine,' she says. 'Washing the dishes!' I can't stand it anymore." Jessamyn shoved her steak to the edge of her tray and nibbled at a forkful of cherry cobbler.

Isn't life ironic? Here I'd just committed the worst crime of my life taking that money, and now all of a sudden—poof!—I'm a Good Influence. It happened at about two o'clock Saturday morning, when Jessamyn's mom came home to find me washing dishes and Jessamyn barfing into the toilet. Mrs. Winter got mad when she saw how much booze there'd been. She actually yelled at Jessamyn.

"She's mad at Nick, too," Jessamyn was saying. "And can you believe it? She's unplugging my phone. For a whole week!"

I shook my head, trying to look sympathetic. Although it was hard to work up a whole lot of sympathy when I couldn't use any phone. And I wasn't even being punished.

"That's not the worst part, either," Jessamyn went on. "She won't let me go skiing next month unless you go, too, being such a Good Influence and all. And I have to go because Nick's meeting me up there, and if I can't, he'll go into his 'come back when you're grown up' act and probably invite some college girl. So now you have to go, Katharyn."

Uh-oh. I plundered my nutty brownie in search of a nut, stalling for time. I'd hoped the ski-trip issue would blow over so I wouldn't have to worry about money for a while. No such luck. Besides, if the ski trips were as much fun as the party had been... My Salisbury steak drifted in a lump to the bottom of my stomach. This Good Influence business was going to cause me grief.

"Katharyn. You can go, can't you?"

"Um, I'm not exactly sure yet."

"You have to."

"I know, but . . ." The lunch-over bell rang, rescuing me for the moment. I jumped up to put away my tray.

"Look, you find out tonight, and I'll call you. Drat! I can't call you. Well, see you after school, anyway. I think you need a pep talk, Katharyn."

It was that kind of day, all day. First off, every single teacher made me stand up in front of the class while they recited my whole name from this little white card. It's amazing how teachers don't stop to think that new kids might not like standing up there while thirty strangers stare holes in their backs. My back happened to be wearing a sweater of 100 percent acrylic, which didn't make me feel any better. I mean, was acrylic out like polyester? Or was it marginally acceptable?

Then I'd have to walk to my seat, with sixty eyes tracking me down the aisle. Now I knew how a whooping crane feels at a bird watcher's convention. After that came the lessons, which weren't quite as bad, but half the time I had no idea what was going on. I was going to flunk out, I knew it.

During my last class, the teacher, Mr. Hawkins, announced we were going to do this original research project on some aspect of local history. "Don't let original research scare you," he said. "We'll discuss how to do it later. For now, choose a partner and get started selecting your topic."

Partners! Oh, wonderful. Original research didn't scare me, not at all, not compared to the prospect of stumbling around and asking—begging—people to be my partner. Chairs scraped, papers rustled and the room filled with talk.

And then something truly horrifying happened. Mr. Hawkins started down the aisle, looking straight at me. I studied the scratches on my desk. I could see what was coming. He asks whether I have a partner, and when I say no, he announces it to the class to get someone to take me, like a charity case. Nobody wants me. There's this long silence in the room while I die an incredibly slow and painful death, and then . . .

"Hi."

I whipped my head around.

"Boy, are you jumpy." It was Kirk.

"You're always sneaking up on me," I said. But I sure was glad to see him. Out of the corner of my eye I saw Mr. Hawkins stop.

"I do not sneak. Hey, I've got a great idea for a topic."

"What?" I asked. Mr. Hawkins turned and walked back up the aisle.

"Your house."

At the front of the room, Mr. Hawkins glanced casually in our direction, then sat down and began shuffling papers.

"Earth to Kate, Earth to Kate. Come in, Kate," Kirk was saying.

"What? Oh, my house."

"Yeah. We can solve the mystery."

"Hmm. Not a bad idea."

"Not bad? It's fantastic!" Kirk grinned. "Besides, this way you'll have to show me your cave."

"All you had to do was ask."

"I know. So we'll check out the wine bottles. Plus anything else you can think of."

"Wait'll you see the photo album. It has pictures of Elise and the doctor and . . ."

"Yeah, you were telling me about those. Pictures of the lantern lady."

"And a trunkful of her clothes. She was really something. Really a neat lady."

"You can tell that, looking at pictures?" Kirk asked. "Or is it in her clothes? Essence of Neat Lady; she was dripping with it, like sweat."

"Oh, shut up. You don't know anything about it." I slugged him, he clutched his arm and rolled his eyes, and before long we got so into talking about Elise and the doctor and the man in white and the whole thing, it seemed as if the bell rang way too soon. Kirk and I walked out of class in the middle of a heavy debate about whether or not Elise was the bootlegging type (I said no; Kirk said yes) and whether or not the doctor was the murdering type (I said yes; Kirk said no).

"Katharyn! Are you coming?" Jessamyn stood by my locker. She tossed her head.

"Ho, boy. Gotta go," Kirk said, and was gone.

Jessamyn looked after him. "I don't mean to say it's your fault, Katharyn. I mean, Kirk's obviously got a thing about you, the way he follows you around. But you're going to have to put an end to it. For his sake."

I felt the flush creeping up my face. "He does not. He's just interested in my house, for a history project."

Jessamyn laughed. "First time I've ever heard that line. Listen, maybe you can't see it, but I can." We walked out the school's front door and headed toward the sidewalk. "I know a thing or two about male psychology. And I'm telling you, he's got the hots for you. You don't want to lead him on, do you?" She turned toward me, one eyebrow delicately raised. "Unless you really like the guy..."

"Not the way you mean. But he's not so bad. I don't know why you..."

An ominous rumble drowned out my words. My heart sank. Belching black smoke, our 1960 Chrysler New Yorker, otherwise known as the Spacemobile, chugged up to the curb. "Katie!" shrieked a familiar, piercing voice. Amy, feet pounding, ponytail streaming, hurled herself at my knees. A mud-caked, piglike creature issued forth, snorted joyfully and waddled in circles around us. This spectacle proved too much for Jessamyn, who lightly sidestepped Cyrano, then joined the onlookers several yards away.

The electric window hummed down. "Hey, Jessie!" called Dad. "Want a ride?"

"No thanks." Jessamyn quickly set off for home.

I'll say one thing for Dad: he can draw a crowd. What with the Spacemobile, the screaming kid and the World's Ugliest Dog, we had practically the whole school staring at us.

"Cut it out, Amy," I said. "Get in the car—quick!"

I slammed the door and slouched in the front seat. The Spacemobile pulled away from the curb with a flatulent bellow. "Dad, what did you have to go and do that for?"

"Do what? What did I do now?"

"Do what? Didn't you see Jessamyn leave? We were going to walk home together! How embarrassing!"

"I thought you liked it when I picked you up from school. You used to like it. Your pal Becky used to like it, too."

"That was in Colorado. Besides, it's okay for little kids. But your parents just don't pick you up when you're in high school. Especially in old junkers like this."

"Old junkers! This is a classic!"

"Oh, right."

After a while, Dad said, "Katie, I wonder about Jessamyn. She's a nice girl, I'm sure, but I wonder if she's, uh, the best friend you could have chosen."

"What's wrong with Jessamyn?" I demanded.

"Nothing's wrong with her. I'm not saying that. But she seems to be influencing you in ways that—that are not altogether beneficial."

"Are you kidding? If it weren't for Jessamyn, I wouldn't have any friends. If it weren't for her, I wouldn't have the faintest idea how to get along in Blue Heron. She's really popular. You don't realize how lucky I am she wants to be my friend."

Dad stared straight ahead and said nothing, which never fails to make my blood boil.

"Well? Aren't you going to say anything?"

"Yes I am." His voice was soft, controlled. "I know you're going through some hard times. So are the rest of us. Your mother stays up late at night, worrying. You've been thoughtless with Amy, who practically worships you. Coming to pick you up from school was her idea this morning. It was going to be a surprise. But you were too concerned with yourself even to be civil. You're going to have to pull yourself together, Kate, and willingly make some sacrifices for the common good."

I felt bad as I thought about Amy plotting all morning to surprise me. But what about me? Why should I have to be responsible for her all the time? Mom was out doing her thing, and Dad was in there tearing the house apart, and that left good old dependable Kate to take care of Amy.

The thing is, I had problems, too. Nobody understood my problems. I couldn't even talk to anybody about them, they were so bad. If only I knew what to do about my own problems, I'd be glad to help with everybody else's. I slumped down farther into the seat, feeling sick and mad and miserable.

When we got home I didn't say anything. I headed upstairs to the turret room. I was in dire need of a fantasy fix. But at the top of the steps I stopped. My feet all of a sudden glued themselves to the floor.

Oh, no!

The room was a jumble of old photos and old clothes strewn every which way on the floor. The lid of one trunk hung lopsided from a single hinge; the other hinge jutted, torn, from the trunk's mouth. It was empty. Inside, the paper lining had been ripped away, exposing bare wood.

"Dad!" I croaked, finally. "Dad, come up here. Quick!"

I pawed through the wreckage for my favorite white cape. It seemed to be all right, except for the lining, which hung limp, held on to the velvet by a few threads.

"Oh my God." Dad stood in the doorway. He strode across the room to a window, wide open. The window next to it had one pane broken; jagged splinters of glass spiked all around. "Stay there, Amy. Kate, hold Amy and Cyrano."

I put my arm around Amy and grabbed Cyrano's collar. We watched Dad pull on a thick rope, tied around the wall between the broken pane and the open window. More rope slid inside through the window. Dad coiled it around his arm, then dropped it. The rope landed with a heavy thud; a spray of glass twitched briefly on the floor.

"Here's how he got in," Dad said.

"Who would do a thing like this?" Now I really felt sick.

"I don't know. But we're going to find out." Dad sounded grim. "This time we're calling the police."

Chapter Nine

Officer Dietz opened the black leather case. "Checking for fingerprints. Want to watch?"

I did. I found a place on the floor where there was no broken glass and sat down. Amy slipped into my lap. We hadn't straightened up because we knew from TV you weren't supposed to disturb the evidence.

Officer Dietz took a black jar and a wide, black brush out of his case. "I'm going to have to make a bit of a mess here," he said.

I looked around at the tangle of clothes and photos on the floor, the mangled trunk, the splintered window where the message had been traced in the dirt.

"That's okay," I said.

Officer Dietz dipped the brush in the powder and swirled it around on a window near the broken pane.

Now it was even blacker than before. The perfect finishing touch for our disaster area decor.

Officer Dietz wasn't my idea of a typical cop. He was young and nice and real polite. He could have made a crack about how dirty the windows were, but he didn't. I wondered if he saw many windows this dirty in Blue Heron.

"See any suspicious spots?" he asked.

Amy and I stood and studied the places where Officer Dietz had brushed the powder. A few spots near the edges looked a little smudgier than the rest, but I sure didn't see any clear prints.

"What about right there?" I pointed to one of the smudges.

"Could be. Let's see." The policeman cut off a strip of wide tape and pressed it on the sill. Then he peeled it off and stuck the tape onto a white card. Now I could see curved lines which vaguely resembled fingerprints on the card.

"Think we've got one," he said. "Though it's not too clear."

"Think you'll get any good ones?"

"Don't know. It's hard to get a clear print when the windows aren't, uh, spotlessly clean to begin with."

"They are pretty dirty," I admitted.

Officer Dietz shrugged. "Oh, well. You just moved in."

He cut off another strip of tape and pressed it to the sill. Yes, Officer Dietz was all right. It was his partner who spooked me. Officer Bradley was short and squat, with a red face and a thick neck. He reminded me of a bulldog. Or a bull, period. He had a way of looking at you as though he wouldn't trust you, no matter what you said.

Right now I heard him talking with Dad out in the hall. "You saw someone out there twice? And the second time he was actually writing on your window? And it never occurred to you to call the police? Why not?"

Dad mumbled something to the effect that he hadn't seen it the first time himself—his fifteen-year-old daughter had. And the second time he only saw a dark shape running away, nothing he could identify in a police lineup.

"That's just great. Do you mind telling me if you planned to take care of the situation yourself? Or did you think it would just go away?"

"As a matter of fact, I did put bolts on all the doors and extra locks on the downstairs windows."

"A fat lot of good they do when you leave the front door unlocked. There's how your burglar got in."

"It's kind of hard to open." Dad sounded sheepish.

"A lot easier than climbing three stories up a rope. That rope is how he got out."

"Look. You know how these haunted house stories get started," I heard Dad say. "I didn't want to give credence to them by calling the police. Yes, there was apparently someone snooping around. But what could you have done about it? No harm was done, and whoever it was would have been long gone by the time you got here. Then there was Miss Watts, but she's…"

"Miss Watts? What Miss Watts? Tell me about Miss Watts."

"She lives across the bay. She called our Realtor and told him she'd seen lights inside the house a week or so before we moved in. But Miss Watts is apparently rather—eccentric. She could have seen the reflection of the moon, kids, anything. We didn't think much of it."

"You mean there were more than three incidents and it never even occurred to anyone to call the police? God save me from stupidity!" Officer Bradley was exploding again. "Now, are you sure there's nothing else you just might have 'forgotten' to mention?"

"There's no need for sarcasm," said Dad quietly.

Silence. Then a big sigh. "Okay," came Officer Bradley's voice, calmer than before. "So where did this Miss Watts say she saw the lights?" The two men's voices faded as their footsteps sounded down the stairs. I was sure glad Dad had to deal with Officer Bradley and I didn't.

The tape made a ripping noise as Officer Dietz pulled it off the glass. "Think we got one," he said. Amy and I pressed close as he smoothed the tape on the paper. This print looked pretty clear to me.

"Now what?" I asked. "Can you find out whose it is?"

"Not yet. It could be practically anyone's. Your mom's, yours, the former owner's, the Realtor's. When we have a suspect we'll check this print against his for confirmation."

"Oh." I'd sort of hoped they could go through their fingerprint files and nab the guy right away.

"You about wrapped?" Officer Bradley charged into the room, Dad behind him.

"Just about. Got one good print, that's all."

"Pack it up, then."

I pried Amy's arms off my legs and started to leave with her. Officer Bradley made me nervous.

"One moment, young lady."

"Me?"

"No, your little sister. Of course you."

"Oh."

"So. You saw this—whatever it was—at the window."

"Yes."

"And it wrote something on that broken pane—what did you say it wrote?"

I hadn't said anything, not to him, anyway, but I didn't think I'd better mention that now. "It's mine," I said.

"It's mine. Uh-huh. So you're standing there and this thing appears and you just stand around while it takes its sweet time writing *I...T...*apostrophe *S...M...I...N...E* on your window."

"I—I was scared and I couldn't really see, you know, what it was, but..." Darn him! He had me stammering already. And for once I was telling the truth. I floundered through the whole window-writing story while Officer Bradley set his sights on me as if I were a target at a police shooting range. Even when I was through he kept on staring at me until finally he let out a little breath and said, "Fair enough. Now what about these footprints your dad was telling me about?"

"Well, Amy and Kirk and I..."

"Kirk?"

"Kirk O'Brien. He lives two doors down. We found them in the bay over that way."

"When was this?" asked Officer Bradley.

"Let me see. Wednesday. Last Wednesday. The day after the night I first saw the light."

"Come on, Jeff. You brought your camera, didn't you?"

"Yes," said Officer Dietz.

"You, too." Officer Bradley jerked his head at me.

"What?"

"You're going to show us those prints. Officer Dietz here is going to take a picture."

"Um, I don't think you're gonna get anything."

"Why not?"

"Ah, the prints sort of got trampled. And," I added quickly, "even if they hadn't you couldn't see anything because the rain washed them out."

"I don't believe this! You get a piece of solid evidence and not only do you fail to report it, you actually destroy it!"

"Now wait a minute. You got the ladder and the lantern." Dad had finally begun to lose his cool. I'd half expected Officer Dietz to come to my rescue, but all of a sudden he was rummaging through his case as though he'd lost his watch or something.

"What happened was, Kirk and I had Amy and Cyrano with us," I said. "By the time we'd had a chance to look around in the bay, they'd completely trampled the prints."

Amy's lower lip began to quiver so I gave her a hug. "It's not your fault, Amy. You didn't know. Anyway, what difference does it make? The rain washed them out, anyway."

"All right, all right." Officer Bradley sounded tired. "So would you mind showing us what's left?"

As a matter of fact, I did mind.

"Watch out for the railing," I warned, leading the two policemen down the slippery wrought-iron stairway. "It's really loose."

The reason I minded was the cave.

Maybe it was the cold air, or maybe the drizzle was beginning to lubricate my brain cells, I don't know which. Anyway, an obvious fact had jut now dawned on me.

I was in trouble. But big.

The three of us squished through slimy leaves on the trail. At about the third switchback, I turned off our property and cut across the hill. No way was I going to let them get near the cave.

The thing is, if Officer Bradley got so mad about our not telling him about the other stuff, just think what he'd do if he discovered I'd found a cave full of Prohibition wine and old coins. He'd put me away for life. And what if he knew I'd sold some of the coins? And the rest were stashed in my purse?

Oh come on, I told myself, even if he did find the cave, how would he know you know about it? And how could he tell there'd been money in there?

At last we arrived at the bay. I was lifting my hand to point out the tracks when my breath suddenly caught in my throat.

There, right in front of me, were footprints. Clear footprints. Only they weren't the prints of some stranger. They were mine. And I knew exactly where they led. Straight back to the cave.

"Those aren't the prints," I gasped as my breath came rushing out all at once. "I mean, the guy with the light didn't make those. I did. I was chasing my dog the other day. See the paw prints? I was following them. Here, you can kind of see where the other prints were. They went back the other way. In the opposite direction. See? Just to this side of the bridge, then they disappeared." I pointed, to make absolutely sure the policemen got the direction right.

Both men stepped into the bay and headed for the bridge.

As I sat down on the bank, my predicament crystallized in my mind for the first time. I was a criminal. At least to the police I was. If they knew what I'd done with the coins.

Meanwhile, another criminal, maybe dangerous, was stalking our property, breaking into our house, looking for something.

The treasure? Could it be someone who knew about the treasure?

But the treasure was only a handful of coins, worth $275, at most.

Then a chilling thought hit.

The man at the coin shop. Maybe the coins were really worth more—lots more. I could tell he'd wanted them. Maybe he would stop at nothing to get them.

But that didn't make sense, either. I'd gone to the shop after I'd seen the lantern, after the hand at the window.

Involuntarily, I turned and looked at the turret. The light was on, and I could see Dad moving around inside. Wait a minute. At night, the lantern man could see me inside the turret. Much more clearly than I could see him. He might have been watching me all this time. Was that why he had searched the turret room and left the rest of the house alone? Because of me?

The police couldn't help, because if I told what I knew they'd arrest me, too. Ha! That would do wonders for my social status in Blue Heron. "There's Kate Hardin," everyone would say. "She would have got life for grand larceny, but they put her on probation because she's a minor." I'd be about as popular as bubonic plague.

I stood and took several deep breaths to keep the nausea down. I'd buy back the coins. That job place, at school. I'd passed it in the administration building. I'd get a part-time job. Then I'd buy back the coins and tell the police, and they'd find the lantern man and I'd be off the hook for good.

By the time Officer Dietz and Officer Bradley returned, I felt a little better. "Find anything?" I asked, my legs steady, my breath well-modulated.

"No. Those prints are pretty well demolished," said Officer Dietz.

"Sorry. We were so excited when we found them, the idea of preserving the evidence slipped my mind."

"Anything else slip your mind?" Officer Bradley was probing again. I met his eyes for a long moment, then mine sort of slid away.

"No. I've told you everything." Lie Number Twenty-two. "But if I find out more..."

"I know. I'll be the first to know." There was an uncomfortable silence while I studied the lake bed and Officer Bradley studied me. "Listen. This person, whoever it is, could be dangerous. So if anything has slipped your mind, you better unslip it. Now."

"I've told you all I know," I lied again.

"Okay." Officer Bradley shrugged. "But don't say I didn't warn you."

The first thing I did when I got back to the house was throw up.

After that I felt better. Not great, but better.

Next, I took the coins out of my purse and hid them in my underwear drawer.

Then I cleaned the turret room. That felt good— sweeping the glass off the floor, scrubbing the black gunk off the windows. I even cut some cardboard and taped it over the broken places. A few of the dresses were hopeless; I stuffed them into a plastic trash bag. Others weren't too bad, like the velvet cape. It wouldn't be too hard to stitch the lining back in.

The photos posed a problem because the album was completely wrecked; the cover was ripped and the paper had just about disintegrated. I flipped through the glossy prints. Elise in a swimsuit. Elise with the doctor. Elise at a party with a whole bunch of people looking at her. I remembered my favorite picture, the one with Elise linking arms with the doctor and the man in white. Where was it?

I flipped through the rest of the photos. Not there. I spread out all the photos on the floor. No luck. It was gone. I tried to think of any other photos that were missing and couldn't. Except—I closed my eyes and saw it—where was the sad little boy in the sailor suit?

Drat! I swept the photos into a pile. Of all the ones to get lost. I didn't care so much about the kid in the sailor suit, but that other one was special. It had probably been swept into one of the trunks or the trash bag. Maybe it was under a trunk. Anyway, I didn't have time to search for it now. I needed my rest. I had a big day ahead of me tomorrow.

I was going after my first real job.

Chapter Ten

The next day at lunch I went to the career place and found a job. I mean, I wasn't actually hired for it, not yet, anyway, but it was the perfect job, part-time at a day-care center for little kids. Best of all, it paid minimum wage, lots more than baby-sitting. I'd buy back the coins and tell the police everything. Then in another three weeks I'd have earned enough for skiing.

All I had to do was get through an interview with someone at the day-care center. The lady at the career place said I was a natural because of my experience baby-sitting Amy.

I practically skipped out of there, feeling better than I had for a week. Tomorrow at lunch I'd find out when the interview would be. I'd already used up half of today's lunch period, so I hurried to the cafeteria and picked up some yogurt.

"Where were you?" asked Jessamyn. She looked up from her sketchbook, then went on drawing.

I ate my yogurt and watched this incredibly sexy ski outfit take shape in her book. "Oh, I had to get some things straightened out."

"Do you know about skiing yet?"

"Well, it's not for certain but . . ." I thought about the day-care center job and smiled, "I think, maybe, it looks good."

Jessamyn snapped her sketchbook shut. "Great! I'll tell Nick! I knew you'd come through, Katharyn."

"I don't really know for sure if I can . . ." I began.

"Of course you can," broke in Jessamyn. "If you want something badly enough, you'll find a way. And you did it!"

I said something profound, like, "I, uh," but then the bell rang, and I had to gulp down my yogurt in a hurry. I didn't get to explain the whole thing to Jessamyn after school because Nick picked her up. And I didn't get to ask Dad about the job because Kirk was there, gawking at the kissing hedge when I got home.

"What's this thing?" he asked, barely glancing at me.

"It's a—a hedge."

"It looks dead."

A dead kissing hedge. Was that some kind of a symbol, like when your English teacher says winter and she really means old age? It didn't bode well for my romantic future in Blue Heron.

We walked up the path to the door, which stuck, naturally, then all of a sudden unstuck. I careered into the entry hall, tripped over Cyrano and collided with

Amy. We all landed on the floor in a heap of legs, arms and drool.

"Must be nice to be loved," said Kirk, grinning his crooked grin.

"It has its moments."

"Up! Up!" Amy implored. I locked my arms around her middle and swung her around as she screamed bloody murder. Then Kirk had to try, and she screamed some more.

"Hey, what's going on here?" Dad appeared in the kitchen doorway, a paintbrush in one hand, spots of white paint all over. He looked like a dalmatian in reverse.

"Hi, Dad. Remember Kirk O'Brien? We're doing that history project I told you about."

"Oh yes, I remember." Dad switched the paintbrush to his left hand and held out his right to shake Kirk's hand. Then he noticed his right hand was all speckled, so he wiped it on his pants. The speckles smeared. Dad shrugged, giving up on the handshake. "So. The history of the house. Say," he added hopefully, "how about a grand tour?"

"Sure. That would be great!" said Kirk, before I had a chance to poke him or telegraph a Meaningful Glance.

Dad's face lit up. "I guess Katie's shown you the front yard already. Did she tell you about the kissing hedge?" Dad winked at me. I died a thousand deaths.

"Kissing hedge? No, she didn't." Kirk gave me a long look. I died two thousand deaths.

"Dr. Mathieson put it up. Probably around 1927. It's some kind of clematis, I think. We'll know by spring, when the blooms come out and…" There was no stopping him now. We trooped all around the house, while Dad held forth on his current favorite subject. Kirk started knocking on walls to discover a secret passageway, and pretty soon Dad got into the act, too. Amy thought it was a great game, and before long the three of them had knocked on every wall in the house. I had a terrible time getting them all moving so we could get to the cave before dark.

"Katie told you about the break-in, of course," said Dad as we entered the turret room.

"The break-in? No, she didn't."

"I didn't have a chance," I said. "I was going to but you were so busy knocking on walls I couldn't get in a word edgewise."

Kirk listened soberly as Dad told what had happened. "Do you think this could have anything to do with that business back in the twenties? The treasure and all?"

"Oh, no. It's just the price of having a prestige home like this. You're a target," Dad said. I jerked my thumb toward the door but Kirk ignored me and stood around talking to Dad some more. When Dad opened one of the trunks, I ran downstairs to stash a flashlight and a hammer in my slicker pockets. On the way back up I heard Dad say, "I'd let you borrow these photos, but Katie would kill me. She's developed quite a fondness for them."

"Could we get outta here before dark?" I yelled up the stairs. "We've got to see the backyard."

"I'd be glad to show you the yard," Dad said as he and Kirk slowly descended, followed by Amy and Cyrano.

"Uh, thanks," Kirk began.

"No thanks, Dad," I said. "We gotta go."

"Well, if you're sure, I'd be glad to . . ."

"We'll let you get back to work, Mr. Hardin," Kirk said. "Thanks again. Hey, why don't we take Amy and Cyrano, so you can concentrate?"

Amy and Cyrano were already out the door. "Watch out for the railing!" I called. Halfway down the wrought-iron stairway Kirk turned to me. "I hardly got a chance to look at the clothes and pictures."

"Look how late it is, practically dark. We'd never have made it to the cave if I didn't get you out of there. Why did you have to encourage him like that?"

Kirk shrugged. "It was interesting. Besides, it's research. We've got to know all that stuff for our report."

I shook my head. "And why did you volunteer to take . . ." I nodded at Amy. "What a pain. What if she tells?"

"Don't worry. I've got it handled." At the edge of the lake Kirk knelt beside Amy, held both her hands and whispered in her ear. She whispered back, a joyful coconspirator. Then she raised her left hand. Kirk said something and she raised her right instead. There followed a covert exchange during which I made out something about "secret" and "solemnly swear" and "Katie's treasure cave." Kirk rose and announced that the secret oath was now consecrated.

"Oh, brother," I muttered.

Persuading Amy to enter the dark cave was a neat trick, involving a hand-off from Kirk to me. Amy was scared and whiney at first but she got over it. By the time we got to the crates she was bragging about how brave she was and demonstrating her dragon-slaying technique. Kirk and I pried open one of the crates and examined the bottles one at a time. They weren't all alike. Some held red wine and some held white, and most had different names on the labels. But they were similar in one respect.

They were all dated 1928 or before.

"A bootleg cache." Kirk's voice was almost a whisper.

"Maybe," I said. "But we still don't know for sure. We've only looked at one crate so far. Besides, they could all have been put here after Prohibition."

"Technically. But you've got to admit that's pretty unlikely. I wish we had time to look at the rest of the bottles."

"But we don't. Not now, anyway. They'll come searching for us if we stay much longer."

"I also wish we knew if this has anything to do with the stuff happening around your house lately. Your ghost."

"Me, too." Boy, did I ever.

When we came out of the cave, I noticed something in Amy's hand.

"What's that, Ames?" I asked.

"It's mine."

"Okay, but what is it?"

"A picture."

"Where'd you find it?"

"In there." Amy pointed to the cave.

"In there? Are you sure?"

"Yeah. On the floor."

"Can I see it for just a minute?"

Amy held out the picture. Smiling up at me from an old, yellow photograph, linking arms with Dr. Mathieson and the dashing man in white, was Elise.

Chapter Eleven

Sorry, it's out of the question." Mom clunked her coffee cup on the table. I'd baked the tuna casserole and washed the dinner dishes in hopes it would put her and Dad in a receptive mood. I even fixed coffee for them. Real coffee, not the freeze-dried stuff. Then I told them about the day-care center job. Clearly. Logically. In a calm tone of voice.

"Would you please tell me why, Mother?" I asked, hanging fast to the conviction that calmness, like virtue, never goes unrewarded.

"Certainly. I work at the lab Monday, Wednesday and Friday afternoons. Tuesdays and Thursdays I have classes. Your father needs all the uninterrupted time he can get to work on the house. We need you to sit with Amy in the afternoons."

"That's not fair!"

"Life isn't fair," Mom said.

"Listen, I've got an idea. Why couldn't Amy go to the day-care center? She'd love it! I'd be there, and..."

"No. She's going to school five mornings a week, which is plenty for a four-year-old. Besides, day-care costs money, and we can't spare any right now."

"But, Jessamyn expects me to go on this ski trip with her and if I can't go, she can't go, and if I could take this job it would solve everything!" When calmness fails, try hysteria.

"Then maybe you and Jessamyn can think of something else to do that weekend. We'd be delighted to have her come over here."

"Oh, great. She'd just love that."

Dad volunteered, "You can baby-sit other kids in the evenings, Katie. You could earn the money that way."

"If you'd just think about it, Dad, you'd realize what a dumb idea that is. I only get..." Mom was glaring at me. "I know, Mom. Hush. Well, I'm tired of hushing! I've been hushing! I just...you guys don't even know what it's like being a kid in this place. You don't...oh, forget it, you'll never understand." I ran upstairs and flopped onto the floor in the turret room.

I hate it when I do things like that. I had it all planned out so I'd stay calm, I wouldn't blow up. And look what happened. I knew they weren't being mean on purpose, but they were just so dumb! You'd think parents would be a little more tuned in to their kids if they cared about them. But mine were so out of touch, they had absolutely no idea what I was going through. Here I was trying to do the right thing, trying to buy back the coins, and they thought I was just being self-ish.

I got to my feet, leaned my forehead against the cool window pane. The darkness outside didn't seem romantic and full of possibilities anymore. It seemed treacherous, crowded with lurking, shadowy things. I had a bad feeling there was someone out there who wanted something, something I had.

Over the next couple of weeks, I only got in deeper. Those dumb ski trips! Jessamyn talked about them incessantly. Her mother took her shopping and bought a whole new outfit plus boots and goggles. I, on the other hand, hoarded up spare change from baby-sitting other people's kids—my paying clientele. I figured by January 29, the first trip, I wouldn't even have enough to buy back the coins I'd sold for my blouse, much less go skiing.

Meanwhile, Jessamyn made elaborate plans for her rendezvous with Nick and asked my advice at every stage. I didn't want to hear about it. I didn't want to think about it. The whole ski-trip business only reminded me what a jerk I was. A jerk for taking those coins in the first place. A jerk for not having the courage to tell Jessamyn I couldn't go.

A jerk for considering another trip to the coin store.

It might have been different if I'd made a bunch of new friends. Some kids talked to me during classes, but they hardly even said "hi" after school or at lunch.

"Don't you get it?" Kirk asked one afternoon. We were following Amy and Cyrano down the gravel path behind our house to the lake. "Jessamyn's stuck up.

When you hang around with her all the time, people figure you're stuck up, too."

"She's not either stuck up. She's been nicer to me than anyone else."

"I'm just telling you how I see it. Look, haven't you ever wondered why Jessamyn hangs on to you at lunch and between classes? It's not your wonderful personality. She doesn't have any other friends. They come to her parties, but that's about it. She uses people, and everybody knows it but you."

"Then they're using her, too! And anyway, she isn't using me," I said. But as a matter of fact, the idea had crossed my mind.

"I don't want to talk about Jessamyn anymore," I said.

"Suits me," Kirk said. "Give me the tape measure." He pulled out the tape and handed it to me. Holding the metal case, with the tape streaming out behind him, Kirk jogged down the cement stairway and jumped onto the lake bed. He swung Amy, then Cyrano onto the lake. They took off through the muck.

Kirk said, "Put your end on the water line."

I lay on my stomach and held the end of the tape just below the gooey gray stuff on the cliff wall. Yuck. But we had to do this because of what I'd found out the other evening at the library. I'd been going through old issues of the Blue Heron newspaper on microfilm and I'd stumbled upon this article about how the lake was going to be dammed up and the water level was going to rise twelve feet. The article ran in March, 1931.

So I'd told Kirk, and he'd gone to see the lake warden, who was a friend of his dad. The warden said, yeah, they did put in a dam in 1932, and it had raised the water level somewhere between ten and twelve feet.

If it were less than ten feet from the current water level to the cave bottom, we'd know for sure the cave was above water in 1928.

"Nine feet, four inches," Kirk said. "That cave was wide open." He tugged at the tape. "You can let go now."

I let go my end, and the tape screamed back into the metal casing. I walked down the stairs and sat at the bottom, my feet dangling over the edge.

So the cave was above water in 1928.

Wow.

Bootleg. A Prohibition stash.

Then I thought of something. "So how come the cave entrance was bricked over?" I said.

Kirk came and stood on the lake bed just below me. "The warden said there were a bunch of old mines around here in the old days. They got bricked over during the sixties to keep kids out."

"Oh." I stared out toward the middle of the lake, letting it sink in. Cyrano was chasing a flock of indignant ducks through the mist. Amy was chasing Cyrano.

Wait a minute.

Something was happening on the far side of the lake. It was hard to see through the fog, but it looked as if a person were hanging from the cliff, in midair. The person dangled there for a minute, then dropped onto the lake bed.

"It's the original dam, the one they put up in '32," Kirk was saying. "It's made of wood blocks, and they take it apart. Kind of like Lego blocks. Then, when they want to fill up the lake, they put it together again. They open up a sluice gate on the other end of the lake to let water in from the river, and it fills up again."

"What's that?" I said softly.

"A sluice gate? It's a gate that lets water in and out," Kirk said.

"No, I mean..."

A person was bobbing across the lake bed now, beating her arms like some kind of grotesque, humanoid crow. I say "her" because I could make out a black dress and a loose, brown coat, which flapped and blurred in the fog.

"The fire department has a team of scuba divers, and they do rescue exercises in the lake," Kirk said. "The warden invited me to come watch. Maybe if you could get off baby-sitting some afternoon and..."

"Shoo! Shoo! Get out!" A squawking voice sounded from the lake bed.

"What the..." Kirk spun around. I jumped onto the lake bed, and then we were both running across the mud.

She's after Amy, I thought. I ran as fast as I could, but it was like running on dry sand, when your feet sink in and your legs burn and you're going so slow it feels like you're running in place.

Then Amy cut and ran toward me, and I saw that the person was really chasing Cyrano. She went straight at him, arms still flapping, only it wasn't working because Cyrano kept following her and getting tangled in her feet instead of running away. I think he wanted to drool on her shoe.

Amy latched on to my leg. "What's the matter?" I yelled.

The person stopped flapping and stared at me. Up close, she looked real old. She had thin lips and the lines on her face were drawn into a permanent expression of disapproval. A pair of small binoculars hung from her neck; baggy wool socks slumped above her hiking boots. "Is this animal yours?" she screeched.

"Yeah. Cyrano, c'mere, boy."

"It just chased off a great blue heron. Do you know what that means? That animal is down here every day, harassing the wildlife. It's a menace! There's a leash law here, you know. I ought to call the authorities!"

"Hey, he never catches anything," I said. "Besides, anybody who lives on the lake can come here. You have no right . . . hey, ouch!" Kirk was grinding his heel on my boot.

"A great blue heron," he said. "They're pretty rare, aren't they?"

I gaped at him.

"Not so rare as remarkable. That bird had a wing-spread over six feet. They ought to be protected, especially in this town. They suffer enough persecution, without that—" here she glared at Cyrano "—that animal murdering them."

"He didn't either . . ."

Kirk cut me off. "Wow, we're really sorry about that. We'll make an effort to keep him away from the wildlife in the future."

The old lady looked somewhat mollified. "You had better," she said. "Otherwise, something will have to be done to stop that animal.'' She looked at me darkly. ''With the authorities, or without.''

She whirled around and tramped back across the lake.

Chapter Twelve

I waited until Amy and Cyrano were well up the path. Then I lit into Kirk. "That lady is totally weird and obnoxious. Where does she get off telling us Cyrano can't come down here? Then you go and take her side. I don't believe you."

Kirk regarded me calmly.

"You hurt my foot!"

Kirk sighed. "Do you know who she is?"

"No, and I don't care if she's the queen of Blue Heron. And don't you go sighing at me, either. Did you hear what she said? She threatened me."

"That was Ida Mae Watts. She's known for being weird and obnoxious. She's also lived there, across from your house, for as long as anybody can remember. She's such an obvious source for our research, I could kick myself for not thinking of her before."

Ida Mae Watts. So she was the Miss Watts who had seen lights in our house before we moved in. Not wanting to forgive Kirk yet, I turned and walked up the path.

"We've got to get on good terms with old Ida Mae," Kirk said. "She could tell us a lot. Maybe she even saw Elise bootlegging."

"She was not bootlegging!"

Kirk grinned and grabbed my hand. I jerked it away.

"You've really got a thing about her, haven't you?" he asked. His light, penetrating eyes, so close now, stirred up a confusion inside my head.

"About who?"

"Elise."

I looked away, feeling strangely unsettled. "Yeah, well, it's not as bad as the thing you have about Jessamyn."

"Jessamyn! Are you kidding? I can't stand Jessamyn."

"Oh yeah? When people can't stand each other as much as you and Jessamyn can't stand each other, there's usually something else going on."

"Something else!" Kirk sputtered. "That's ridiculous."

"So why do you hate her so much?"

"I told you, she's a phony. She uses people. She…" Kirk kicked at the ground, spewing gravel into the bushes. Head down, hands in his pockets, he shuffled along. "She used me, once."

I walked beside him for a decent interval, until I couldn't contain myself any longer. "How?" I asked.

Kirk shrugged. "Oh, there was this dance. In eighth grade. Jessamyn's mom and my mom have been friends forever, and Jessamyn's mom let my mom know that Jessamyn wanted me to ask her. So I did." He shook his head. "I was pretty excited about it. What a jerk."

"Why? Didn't she go?"

"Oh, yeah, she went. Only the reason she wanted to go with me was to get this other guy jealous. And it worked. The other guy got jealous, asked her to dance, and that was that. She was gone. When I tried to cut in on them, pointed out she was my date, they seemed to think it was real funny."

"Oh." I paused. "I'm sorry."

"Well, live and learn." Kirk looked up at me. "So now it's your turn. What's with Elise?"

"I don't know. I can't explain it."

"Try."

"I don't know. She was beautiful, rich, charming. All that." I glanced quickly at Kirk, then away again. "Everything I'm not."

"So you're not rich. Who cares? And charm takes a while to develop. Or so they tell me. I wouldn't know."

I smiled. "You can say that again." It had started to rain gently. I pulled up my hood, grateful for an excuse to hide the perverse agitation I was feeling.

"You're not half bad-looking, either," Kirk said.

"Oh, right. The Teenage Toothpick."

"You'll fill out. All women do. Then they long for the old toothpick days for the rest of their lives."

"Well, what about this nose?"

"What about it?"

"Oh, come on. It's huge, that's what."

"Hmm." Kirk yanked down my hood and dramatically inspected my nose. My scalp tingled near where his hand had brushed against my hair. "It is slightly aquiline, now that you mention it," he said.

"Aquiline. That's a polite word for gigantic."

"All the Renaissance beauties had noses like yours. Ever look at a Titian or a Botticelli? Or Da Vinci. The Mona Lisa!"

"In case you haven't noticed, the Renaissance is over."

"Okay, so you have an enormous nose." I gave him a swift elbow to the ribs. Kirk dodged, then grabbed for my arm, pulled me close. "Still, it goes with your personality," he said. "You're not the button-nose type." He let go of my arm and grinned. "Your problem is you don't have enough class to appreciate yourself."

"Gee, thanks. You're a real silver-tongued devil, aren't you?"

"Charm. Pure charm."

But later, wearing my cape in the tower room during my nightly fantasy fix, I thought I saw freckles on my tall dark stranger's face. And then I noticed something odder still.

His ears stuck out.

Chapter Thirteen

That night, Cyrano disappeared.

Mom usually lets him out at about ten, and a few minutes later he's back at the door, scratching to be let in.

But this time, he didn't scratch. I found out after I heard Mom yelling for him outside while I was upstairs doing my homework. At first I didn't think much about it, but when the yelling kept up, it began to sink in that something abnormal was going on.

Since I was stuck on my math anyway, I went downstairs to check things out. What I saw was Dad getting into his jacket and Mom still out there yelling for Cyrano.

"What's the matter? Cyrano gone?" I asked with my usual keen deductive powers.

"Yeah." Dad zipped his jacket. "He's probably out there chasing ducks again."

Right then I got a real strange feeling, but I didn't say anything yet. I went back up to my room and gazed in the general direction of my math book for a while. The numbers sort of floated in front of my eyes, but I wasn't thinking about cosines or tangents. I was thinking about Ida Mae Watts, about what she had said that afternoon. After a while I gave up on math and went downstairs to wait with Mom.

Dad was gone an hour. By that time Mom and I were beyond working the newspaper crossword puzzle and pretending nothing was the matter; we had stationed ourselves in the living room, near the door.

Which now flew open, and Dad came in, alone.

"I don't get it," he said. "I searched all over the darn place. In the lake. Up the road. I honestly don't think he's out there." He bent to unlace his boots.

"I just don't get it," he muttered.

"I think . . . I might," I said.

I told them about Ida Mae. At first they acted as I'd expected they would—adults have this code, like in the Mafia, where they protect their own, no matter what. They said she couldn't possibly have done anything to Cyrano, she hadn't been threatening, that's just the kind of thing people say when they're frustrated, stuff like that. I didn't push it. After all, we had no proof, it was only a possibility. But I caught Mom and Dad looking at each other sideways a couple of times.

"I'm sure he'll turn up in the morning," Mom said. But I could see she was worried.

To tell the truth, so was I.

Cyrano didn't turn up in the morning.

It was a crummy day all around. I felt sick about it, and to make things worse, this was also the day I'd decided to back out of the ski trips with Jessamyn.

"What are you saying to me!" demanded Jessamyn when I finally got up my nerve at lunch. "Katharyn, if I didn't know better I'd think you don't want to go skiing."

"Oh, I do. It's just that..."

"You made a commitment. Now you're saying you can't go, and the first trip's a week from tomorrow. You know how important these trips are to me. I thought I could count on you."

"I didn't really say for sure I could go."

"Is it your parents?" Jessamyn asked. "Tell them you have a right to live your life, too. It isn't fair for them to keep you locked up in that hideous old house all the time."

"I know it's not fair but what can I do?"

"You're going to have to learn to deal with them like I do with mine. Stand up to them! If you really want to go, you'll find a way. If you can't, I guess you just don't care enough to be my friend." Jessamyn slammed down her Diet Pepsi, got up from the table and walked out.

Kirk's words came back to me: "She uses people, and everybody knows it but you." I shut them off. I thought of those coins just sitting there in my underwear drawer and came to a decision.

I would sell the rest of the coins. The man could just have them if he wanted them so badly. It was no big deal.

Cyrano didn't turn up that afternoon.

Kirk did, though. He stopped by to see if Cyrano had come back yet, then he asked the obvious question.

"Don't you think it's strange that Cyrano disappeared the day after old Ida Mae threatened him?" he asked.

I gave him what I hoped was a sufficiently scathing look.

Kirk ignored it. "We're going to have to investigate this thing," he said.

"Oh, we are, are we?"

"Hey, I'm just trying to help. I kind of like old de Bergerac. I thought, since he's your dog, you might care about him, too."

I sighed. "Okay. What kind of investigating are we going to do?"

The kind of investigating was, we tell our parents we were going to the library that night, but really we snoop around Ida Mae's house. If Cyrano were there, he might smell us or hear us and bark or snort or something. It sounded good, in theory, except it was one more lie. I mean, unless Ida Mae had done something worse to Cyrano than just dognapping, which was a possibility I didn't even want to think about.

But that night as we sneaked across the lake bed, I began to see the practical drawbacks of the plan. For one thing, it was cold out and raining, or more like heavy misting. Plus the lake was downright treacherous in the dark. You couldn't pick your way because even with a flashlight it was impossible to judge whether your next step would land you on dried-out mud or in the real goopey stuff.

"Come on!" Kirk whispered. Now he'd reached the metal ladder behind Ida Mae's house, the one she'd come down yesterday. It looked pretty stable; the only problem was it ended about four feet above the lake bed.

Kirk swung up onto the ladder. I grabbed on, jammed one boot against the bottom rung, then managed to haul myself up.

The ladder felt cold; grit and mud from Kirk's boots oozed between my fingers. I craned my neck to see past Kirk to where the ladder ended. I knew for sure that when he got there we'd be discovered by a pack of ferocious Dobermans, which Ida Mae kept especially for mauling trespassers.

Kirk reached the top. The silence roared loud in my ears.

No Dobermans.

He crouched way down low and ran across the back lawn. He flattened himself against the house, pointed his flashlight straight up. I beat it across the lawn and stood beside him. My flashlight beam was jumping all over the grass because my hand was shaking. Why did I ever let him talk me into this?

"Now what?" I whispered.

"Turn off your flashlight. Follow me."

Slowly, stooping when we passed windows, we stole toward the front of the house. I strained my ears to pick up any sound of Cyrano, but all I could hear was a sort of garbled chattering: the TV. We tiptoed past the front of the house in full view of the street. My heart was drumming wildly; if anyone saw us, it would be all over.

Then, just as we reached the other side of the house, I heard a soft "click."

I froze. Kirk did, too. I stood there, my feet rooted to the ground, hardly daring to breathe. We looked at each other, then began to scan the darkness. A tree. A fence. A bush.

All still. All silent.

It felt as if we stood there for hours, but it couldn't have been more than a minute or two. Then Kirk looked back at me, shrugged and tiptoed forward. Toward the back of the house was a basement window with one of those metal wells around it. Kirk got down on his hands and knees; he tugged at the window.

"Give me some light, would you?" he whispered.

I crouched and shone my light on the window. Kirk wobbled the window a few times; there was a sudden crack and it slammed wide open.

I shone my light into the basement. "Cyrano!" I whispered. "Are you there, boy?"

There came a faint whistling noise, then another crack, a louder one. Kirk moaned and collapsed on the ground.

Chapter Fourteen

I screamed.

The whistling noise came again, and a black blur zoomed in toward my face. I rolled over, crouched, facedown, my arms protecting my head. Something crashed on the ground beside me.

When I looked up again, everything was happening like a movie slowed way down to where it's freeze frames. Hiking boots with baggy wool socks. A brown coat with fuzzy little pills on it. A tattered umbrella.

Mary Poppins, I thought, absurdly. Some kind of weird, malevolent Mary Poppins.

The umbrella rose again. I squatted there, my eyes glued to it, waiting for it to come crashing down.

The umbrella quivered a long moment. Then, slowly, it lowered to the ground.

"It's you!" croaked Ida Mae Watts.

She jabbed the umbrella at Kirk. "See if he's all right," she said.

I crawled over to Kirk and felt for a pulse on his wrist the way we'd been taught in health class. I never could find a pulse, not even on my live victims in class. I pressed my thumb hard against Kirk's wrist but all I could feel was my own trembling, no pulse underneath. He's dead, I thought. I know it. Oh no, he's dead for sure.

Kirk moaned.

"Wha...what happened?" He sat up. He blinked a bunch of times then looked down at his wrist, which I was still holding.

"I thought you were...someone else." Ida Mae sounded uncertain. Then she turned toward me. This seemed to revive her. "What are you doing here?" she demanded. "You have no business on my property."

Kirk was still looking at his wrist. I moved to take away my hand, but he grabbed it and held on.

I licked my lips, trying to cut through the confused whirling going on in my head, trying to zero in on a plan of action. Kirk was definitely alive. But I wasn't so sure he was up to the walk back. Anyway, if we could get into the house, we might be able to find Cyrano. "Look," I said. "Kirk's obviously not feeling so hot, so could we please go inside and rest a moment?"

Ida Mae's black eyes darted from me to Kirk and back to me again. Then she turned on her heel and stalked off toward the front door. At the corner of the house she whipped her head around. "Are you coming," she rasped, "or not?"

Inside, a sweet stuffiness hung in the air, like my grandmother's lavender perfume.

"Drink," Ida Mae commanded.

She set two steaming cups of tea on the coffee table. This was no mean feat, because a flock of tiny ceramic birds with crocheted doilies for nests inhabited practically every square inch.

Kirk inhaled a huge gulp of tea. He had revived admirably for someone who'd just been knocked silly by a vicious umbrella. While Ida Mae was making tea in the kitchen, he'd kept me talking continuously on the theory that if Cyrano were here and heard me, he'd bark or snort or otherwise make his presence known.

No such luck.

I lifted the teacup, inhaled its steam.

"Chamomile," Ida Mae said to me.

I forced myself to smile. The tea had a sickly, sourish taste to it.

"Do you know what they did to trespassers when I was a youngster?" Ida Mae said, her voice thin and angry.

Kirk, to my disgust, actually began telling her what we'd been doing. I couldn't believe it. He didn't know what that woman would do to us—or to Cyrano, if he were here.

Ida Mae sniffed. "If you think I'd permit that animal anywhere near my home, you're sadly mistaken," she said. "Although I can't say I'm sorry it's gone."

"Who could have taken him?" Kirk asked.

"What makes you so sure somebody took it? It probably just ran away."

"Cyrano wouldn't do that," I said.

Ida Mae crooked a talonlike finger as she brought her teacup to her lips. Perched on a small, high-backed chair covered with needlepoint, she looked strangely out of place. A crow in a hummingbird's nest. Something about this house—all the dainty little things around this definitely undainty person—made me feel uneasy. It seemed warped, out of whack.

"Maybe it was the guy with the lantern," Kirk said.

Ida Mae's teacup clattered against her saucer. "How did you know about that?"

"Kate saw the lights. Didn't you, Kate?"

I nodded.

"Kate's Realtor said you saw them, too."

Ida Mae gazed past me, half smiling. Her eyes glazed over; the harsh lines in her face softened. All at once she seemed younger, gentler. I turned to see where she was looking and noticed, for the first time, the view from the window at the back of the room. Centered in the window, framed like a painting with a foreground of lake and a background of trees, stood our house.

"I see you at night, sometimes," she said in a soft, almost dreamy tone of voice. "Up there, in the tower. At first I thought you were . . . someone else."

I shivered suddenly. "Elise," I whispered.

"Yes," she said. "But you're not." Her gaze, still unfocused, brushed across my face. She held a small, ceramic bird cupped in one hand. Her bony thumb caressed the bird, followed the curve of its neck and down across the hard, shiny feathers on its back. "She wasn't a very nice person, you know. She was immoral."

"How do you know?" I blurted.

"Oh, I know." Ida Mae jerked her head away from the window; she looked straight at me. "I watch birds. And other things."

I remembered the small binoculars hanging from her neck when we'd seen her on the lake bed, and I felt cold all over. This woman was strange.

"I don't believe it," I said. "She wasn't like that."

Ida Mae smiled slyly. "Oh, yes. Yes she was. In many, many ways. She drank. Liquor. It was illegal then, you know. But I was willing to forgive her that. Even though she shouldn't have. People should watch what they do in front of people who look up to them. Especially young people, people who want to be like them. They should set a good example. Not disappoint other people." The hand not holding the ceramic bird hovered over it, spindly fingers stroking, feather-light. "But still, the drinking was forgivable. Then she became acquainted with Mr. John Calais."

Ida Mae looked past me again, as if she'd retreated to some private place inside. I waited, not knowing if she were through or not, wondering if she expected me to say something. But soon she went on. "I was engaged to care for his son, Dion, when Calais came to visit the Mathiesons. He often brought Dion, but Mrs. Calais never came. I was twelve. Dion was five. So I was right there when the goings-on began between Mr. John Calais and *her*."

Ida Mae fell silent again, but her hand kept on stroking the ceramic bird.

Kirk said, "Who was John Cal..."

"How he treated that boy." Ida Mae spoke as if she hadn't heard Kirk at all. "That Dion. Him always trying to please his father. And his father always making fun of him. They called him the gentleman bootlegger, but that man was cruel. He was evil. Why, one time he lifted Dion by the feet and held him over the water upside down. Dion was terrified of water. Calais laughed. Just laughed and laughed. *She* laughed with him. Dion was hysterical for an hour after that."

A picture clarified in my mind, like a Polaroid photo developing. A sad-faced boy in a sailor suit.

"The gentleman bootlegger?" Kirk was saying. "You mean Calais was bootlegging?"

Ida Mae's eyes jerked from the window to Kirk, then to me. "I think you know," she said to me. "Don't you?"

My throat closed up. I couldn't say a word.

"Well, it doesn't matter, I guess. Not anymore. Too many years... Yes, there was bootlegging. I didn't believe it myself, until... Oh, Calais, I knew about him, but *her*... I guess it was for the money. She had exquisite clothes. And parties, yes, yes, the parties. They used to dance and dance." Ida Mae began to hum. She hummed softly to herself, staring off into the distance, fondling the ceramic bird. She swayed gently in her chair, back and forth, back and forth.

The back of my neck prickled. Kirk raised his eyebrows at me.

"I used to hear her arguing with Dr. Mathieson about money," Ida Mae said. "Then the arguments ended but the clothes and the parties kept coming."

"I heard them talking one night in the garden. Calais and *her*. 'We're coming for the wine tonight,' he said. She asked if she could keep a case, and he said no. 'You're being paid in other ways, my dear,' he said. And then they..."

Ida Mae closed her eyes, bowed her head and touched her temples with her fingers. The ceramic bird lay still in her lap. When she spoke again her voice was harsh. "So I telephoned the police. People shouldn't be allowed to carry on like that. I saw her running down the hill when the police were searching the house. She got into a boat. The police never found anything. Even though she was gone, they didn't believe me, what I heard. They patted my head. They said it was my imagination. The fools! The police are fools! Let them try to solve that case themselves." She paused and looked hard at me. "But I found something. You did, too. I know about that."

My heart pounded so loudly I knew everyone in the room must hear. I held my breath, waiting for the accusation, waiting for her to say she'd seen me take the coins. But she seemed to drift on to another thought.

"He died, you know," Ida Mae said. "Just last week."

"Who died?" I exhaled.

"Calais. Here." She stood, set the bird on the coffee table and walked to the fireplace. She picked up something from the mantle and handed it to me. A newspaper clipping.

"The End of an Era," the headline said. The paper made a big deal about it, actually. The story went into the whole bootlegging thing, plus the history of Calais's life. The gentleman bootlegger. After all that money he had, he'd died poor. But it was the pictures that got me. Because I knew Calais.

Calais was the man in the white suit.

Chapter Fifteen

She didn't necessarily do it," I said. I yanked on the hood of my slicker, trying to keep the light rain off my face as we walked down the street toward home. I was not feeling well.

"Nope," Kirk said. "Cyrano wasn't in that house."

"I mean Elise. Just because she left that night doesn't make her a bootlegger. Maybe the doctor was mean to her. Maybe he beat her."

"Oh, so that's what's bugging you." Kirk shook his head so slightly you'd hardly notice. I noticed. It's a good thing he didn't say "I told you so," or anything like that. I would have wrung his neck.

"Maybe Calais was helping her escape," I said.

Kirk didn't answer. Cold penetrated my left foot where I'd stepped in a puddle, and water leaked into my boot. I pulled my slicker tighter around me.

"I don't trust that Watts lady anyway. She's warped. Maybe she made up the whole thing."

"She didn't make up the whole thing. We found the wine, remember?"

I remembered.

"Listen, Kate. Maybe Elise wasn't involved, but even if she was... You've read about Prohibition. Everybody was doing it. Everybody was breaking the law in one way or another. It was the thing to do. So even if she was involved, it was no big deal. She got caught, that's all. It was no big deal."

No big deal. So how come it felt like a big deal? How come I cared whether Elise was bootlegging or not? What was she to me?

The rain really started thwacking down. Cold trickled through my shoulders, seeped way down deep inside my back. We were going home around the lake. I couldn't face that lake bed again.

If I really wanted to feel rotten, I told myself, I shouldn't be thinking about something that happened more than half a century ago. I should be thinking about Ida Mae Watts and how much she knew. How much she saw with those little bird-watching binoculars. Like had she seen me take the coins? Had she guessed that I had sold them?

I winced, thinking about the suspicious way the man at the coin store had looked at me when I came on Friday to sell the remaining coins.

And if Ida Mae did know, would she tell? That was worth feeling rotten about.

That, plus Cyrano. He was worth feeling rotten about, too.

Kirk said goodbye at the kissing hedge, and I ran upstairs to the tower room.

"Katie! Katie! Guess what happened?" Amy pounded up behind me.

"Amy, I don't want to play. Isn't it past your bed time?"

Amy stood there a minute looking at me. Her lower lip quivered. Then she walked slowly back down the stairs.

You jerk, I told myself. You jerk, you jerk. I ransacked the trunk for the white cape and draped it over my shoulders. No, that won't do. I shrugged off the cape, stripped off my jeans, my shirt, my wet boots. Then I stepped into a long, silk dress and shoes with silver threads. Cold. I felt cold. Get the cape. I flung it on, closed my eyes and twirled around, hoping to stir up the magic that always came when I dressed up like Elise. But looking back from the mirror was only me, Kate Hardin, looking angry and sad and too old for dress-up. I shivered.

The magic was gone.

"It's no big deal!" I shouted at the mirror. So what if I sold those coins? I was forced into it.

Right. Just like Elise was forced into bootlegging.

I sank to the floor in a heap of silk and velvet and fur. All at once I knew why it mattered so much whether Elise had been bootlegging or not. Because I'd wanted to be her. I'd tried to become her. And now it turned out the her I'd tried to become was...not such a hot person.

If the bootlegging part were true, probably all the rest was true, too. She went into debt for parties and clothes. She yelled at her husband because he didn't give her what she wanted. She laughed at that little kid.

Downstairs, a door slammed; there were voices. They sounded faraway, unreal.

Maybe, it occurred to me, maybe this house really was haunted. Haunted by Elise. I'd called her back; I'd asked her to help me be like her.

And she had. Boy, had she ever.

Except it wound up like those fairy tales where you get three wishes and they come true in ways you'd never imagined. I didn't get popular or beautiful. But I did fall into the same traps that caught Elise. The trap of thinking you need money to be popular. The trap of getting so obsessed with popularity, you value the wrong people and neglect the ones who count.

A flurry of creaking and pounding sounded on the stairs. A fat, furry missile hurtled onto my lap. It licked my face. It snorted.

"Cyrano!"

"A lady found him! She called, and Dad went to get him!" Amy was panting. "Aren't you just so happy!"

"What's the occasion? Is this for Cyrano?" I asked, as Mom carried a cake to the table. It had little rose-buds all around, but no words to clue me in.

"Not exactly," Dad said. "Your mom and I have some good news. I talked to my agent today, and it looks as if he may have found a home for the book. With a much bigger advance than the one we gave up. If it goes through we'll get a phone, and you can buy some clothes. We'll start paying your baby-sitting bills, too."

"It's still a maybe," warned Mom. "But we thought we'd splurge a little tonight, anyway."

"That's great, Dad. Congratulations."

It dawned on me how hard this advance business must have been for him. Going ahead with his book with no guarantee of it ever being published. Not being able to provide for his family, something I've heard is very traumatic for adult males. Plus getting a lot of static about money from me.

Dad beamed. "We won't be on easy street, don't get me wrong. But it looks as though the pinch is going to ease up." He made a little flourish with the knife before sinking it into the cake. "My agent is flying out tomorrow, and Mom and I are meeting him for lunch. Don't worry, Katie. I know that's when you're leaving for your ski trip. We've already hired a sitter to take care of Amy when you go."

Those dumb ski trips! I didn't even want to go anymore. I'd lied to my parents again about them, said they were paid for by a rummage sale at the school last fall.

Yeah, I was glad about the new book contract. Glad for Dad. Glad for me. We'd get a phone now, and the remodeling would go faster. I could buy some socially acceptable clothes.

I was going to survive, here in Blue Heron.

But the whole thing with the coins and the secrets and the lies was like a poison burning away inside me, spoiling my happiness.

Saturday morning, the day of the first ski trip, my hair didn't come out. When I unrolled my electric rollers, it stuck out spastically every which way.

"Let's play Cootie," suggested Amy for the forty-eighth time that morning.

"I can't. Look at my hair! They'll be here any minute. What am I gonna do?"

"But you promised."

"I know I did. And I'm sorry. Look, we'll play Cootie as many times as you want when I get back tomorrow night."

Amy sighed. "Let's go, Cyrano." They clattered down the hall.

Outside, a horn blasted.

Oh, no. Nick and Jessamyn. Already! Nick was driving us to the ski bus so Jessamyn's mother wouldn't suspect he was meeting her on the mountain. The tearful goodbye scene and all that.

"I'll be right out," I yelled through the window. I took a last, desperate swipe at my hair, grabbed my duffel bag and tore out into the pouring rain.

"Hurry!" Jessamyn said. "Let's go!"

"The sitter's not here yet," I said, shoving my bag into the back seat. "I have to wait till she comes."

"Oh come on! Amy's a big girl. She can wait here alone for a few minutes."

"Nope. Can't do that. The sitter'll be here soon."

Jessamyn rolled her eyes and tapped her fingers on the door handle. "If she doesn't get here right away we'll miss the bus!"

"She'll be here soon. She was due five minutes ago."

"Five minutes! I bet she forgot! You better call her."

"I suppose I could, but . . ."

"Do it, Katharyn! I've got to get on that bus! Come on!"

"Well, okay." Crashing through the front door, I called out, "It's just me, Amy." No answer. "Amy?" Still no answer.

I ran upstairs to her room. She wasn't there. Then back down to the family room. No Amy.

"Amy, you come here this minute! I don't have time for games!" Still no answer. I tore through the house, checking Amy's secret hiding places. No luck. Where else could she be except outside? And she wouldn't go out in this downpour. Unless... Come to think of it, I hadn't seen Cyrano around, either. I raced upstairs again and checked out the coat pegs on Amy's wall. The wool coat was there. The pink and blue sweaters were there. But the yellow peg where she usually hung her slicker stood empty.

"Oh no."

Back at the car, Jessamyn's words came in an angry stream. I let them wash over me. "I can't leave yet," I said. "Amy's gone."

The stream of words surged louder. "I can't believe you'd do this to me. This is it, Kate. This is absolutely the end." I took my bag from the back seat. As I reached the front door, Nick's car zoomed away.

The red taillights streaked like ribbons on the wet street.

Goodbye, Jessamyn.

I cut through the house and sped down the wrought-iron stairway.

"Amy!" I should have put on my slicker. I realized this halfway down the switchbacks. My ski jacket was

already soaked. And no hood. Rain splashed on my
face and hair.

"Amy!" I ran across the hill toward the bay where
we'd seen the footprints. Amy wouldn't go out for no
reason. She must have gone after Cyrano. And it
didn't take a genius to figure that Cyrano would head
straight for the ducks.

"Amy!" A trickle of water ran down my neck and
under my collar. My jacket hung on me like a weight.
I stumbled on a rock; my ankle turned.

I froze. What I saw chilled me far, far more than the
rain.

Chapter Sixteen

Water. The bay stood half-full of water. More water churned under the bridge, smacked into itself, roared to get to the lake, and there it was, my old water nightmare, back again.

I yanked off my shoes and plunged into water past my knees. I had some insane idea of chasing through the bay after Amy. But the current slammed into my legs, the roaring filled my ears and in my head I saw Amy trying to stand in this, getting knocked down, struggling to her feet, getting knocked down again and . . .

"Amy!" I screamed. "Where are you!"

I stood there as long as I could stand it, scanning the bay. Nothing. No moving shapes in the gray water.

I clambered out and put on my shoes. Something cold nuzzled my hand. Cyrano! My heart leapt.

"Cyrano, where's Amy? Go get Amy!" He snorted. "Fetch!" I shouted hysterically. He waddled around me, wagging his tail, as if I'd invented a new game.

Cyrano followed me up the hill. My right ankle throbbed. Gravel scrabbled out from under my feet. I slipped, fell and came down on my palms. Dimly I noticed the blood; it didn't matter, I was up and going again. Then it hit me, just as I reached the switch-back trail.

The cave. She wouldn't have gone to the cave.

Or would she?

Downhill now. I was so drenched I could hardly feel the rain. At the foot of the hill, I stopped. The concrete platform and the bottom steps were gone. In their place was water. Dark gray water slid knee-deep into the mouth of the cave. Cyrano whined; he couldn't get in. But I could.

Fighting panic, I crawled through the water into the cave.

"Amy, are you in here?"

My voice echoed. Then came another, smaller, fainter. "Katie. I'm here."

"Oh, Amy." My knees went to mush; I leaned against the cave wall. Then I was climbing up as fast as I could. I didn't notice when I wasn't wading through water anymore; I didn't even notice the glow in the passageway. All I could think about was Amy.

There she was. Sitting on a rock. But even as I reached for her I knew something was wrong. She didn't hug me back. I felt the ropes knotted at her wrists at the same time I heard the voice.

"Well, well, well. Looks like we've caught our thief."

I spun around. Yellow light painted the man's face; sinister shadows danced across it. In one hand he held a lantern.

"Where is it?" the man demanded.

"What?"

"Don't play games with me." He jerked his head toward Amy. "She told me Katie was gonna come find her. She told me this is Katie's treasure cave. You're Katie. So where's the treasure?"

I stared at him.

"Where is it?" The man lurched toward me.

"In my room!"

"Ah." He visibly relaxed. "So the old man was telling the truth." He put down the lantern and squatted on an outcrop of rock. Without the harsh yellow glare his face didn't look sinister so much as—puffy. Puffy eyelids, puffy jowls. Grayish hair puffing out around his head. He muttered to himself, smiling. Something about an inheritance.

I wrapped my arms around Amy and murmured into her ear. "It's gonna be all right." Although, to tell the truth, I wasn't so sure. Splintered wood littered the cave floor; shards of glass glittered in the light. The wine crates, the bottles, were gone.

"My feet hurt," said Amy. I held her at arm's length and looked down. Her ankles were tied together. A pool of something dark and red stained her shoes. I touched it with my finger and sniffed. Wine.

Abruptly the man stood and turned as if he'd just remembered us. "Okay. Let's go."

"Better untie Amy first."

"Amy? Oh, her. She's not coming."

"Not coming? You're crazy! What about the water? She'll be trapped if she's not coming."

"Oh, you're real bright. You figured that out all by yourself," he said. "But what if you don't feel like leading me to the treasure? What if you take me on a wild-goose chase? Or yell for help? This way you'll be a good girl and get right to it. 'Cause we'd hate to have little Amy trapped in the cave, wouldn't we?"

My heart pounded in my ears. "Look," I said reasonably. "I won't call for help. I promise, okay?"

"Let's go," he repeated.

"No. I won't. Not without Amy."

The man sighed. "Okay. We'll do it the hard way." He jammed a puffy hand into his coat pocket and rummaged around. Out came two pencil stubs, a handful of gumdrops and a stiff piece of paper. Then the hand again, holding a gun.

I was very calm about the gun, for me. The paper distracted me. It had fallen to the ground by the lantern. In the yellow light I could see that it wasn't a piece of paper, after all. It was a photograph. And all at once everything came clear for me. I knew who the man was.

The image of a sad-faced, five-year-old boy in a sailor suit flickered in the light. "You're Dion Calais," I said.

"Get moving."

"You're the bootlegger's son."

"Right. And that treasure's *mine*. The old man told me, there's treasure hidden at the old Mathieson place. And if I can find it, it's mine. My inheritance. He gave me his old bootlegging lantern. For luck, he says. Huh! Luck! I ain't never had no luck."

He gave the lantern a quick jab with his foot. I held my breath. It teetered to one side, then tipped back up. "The dumb thing broke, that's my luck. I had to go out and spend good money for this piece of junk."

"I looked for weeks. I even found this cave, but no treasure." Dion pointed his gun at me like an accusing finger; his voice became petulant, almost childish. "You stole it. It's my inheritance!"

I swallowed hard.

"I saw you up there, in that tower. Putting on airs. At first I thought you were her, the one that used to laugh at me. But she went away. I knew you were up to something, so I kept my eye on you."

"You broke in and..."

"I wasn't taking no chances on you grabbing my inheritance. But then the old man had a heart attack, and I had to get back up to Seattle. And I made him tell me. Before he died he told me. 'It's in the cave you found,' he says. 'Look harder.' So I did. I even smashed all the bottles to see if it was inside one of them. But it wasn't. You got it. So I figured, take the dog, ransom it off, but the thing escaped. But then I got her." Dion jerked his head toward Amy. "And now—" Dion smiled in a way I didn't like at all "—now I got you."

He stuffed the gun into his pocket, took hold of my jacket and shoved me back down the passageway. Amy began to cry. At first I kicked and elbowed and tried to dig my fingernails into the wall but it didn't do any good. Dion was too strong. "Amy! I'll be back!" I yelled. When I crawled through the cave opening I had to close my mouth, the water was that deep.

"Move it," said Dion. He grabbed my jacket and pushed me again. I stumbled up the slippery steps and struggled up the hill. I was soaked, and my ankle tingled every time I came down on my right foot. Dion let go of my jacket, but every so often he gave me a shove. He kept muttering to himself about "treasure" and "my inheritance." I felt panic rising inside me.

The treasure was gone. It hadn't been much of a treasure to begin with, but I had sold it, all there was. All that was left was an empty box and about thirteen dollars. When Dion found out...

I had to get back to Amy. I had to, no matter what.

Halfway up the wrought-iron stairway, I stopped. "Oh, no!" I cried, pointing back across the lake. "Look!"

It worked. Dion spun around to face the lake. "I don't see..." he began.

I sucked in my breath and shoved.

I hit him in the chest. The shrill, grating sound came once more as the wrought-iron railing broke loose from the post. Dion, an astonished look on his face, toppled backward in slow motion. He disappeared over the cliff.

I ran.

Down the steps, around the switchbacks, over the dock, my screams for help echoing behind me. At the edge of the cement steps to the lake I slipped and came down wrong on my right foot. Unbelievable pain zigzagged up my leg. I got up, took a step and staggered.

"Amy!" I called. I held my breath and crawled through the cave opening, through the water. "Are you okay?"

"Ye-es." She hiccupped in the middle of the "yes," one of those hiccups you do when you've been crying.

"I'm coming. Don't worry. But I hurt my foot so it might take a while."

"That's okay. Does it hur(hiccup)urt?"

"Not really." Lie Number 103.

"Katie?"

"Yes?"

"Would you please keep talking?"

"Of course, Ames." I talked about Aquaman as I limped through the water at the bottom of the cave. I talked about Wonder Woman as I crawled up the passageway. I talked about how the police were going to rescue us as my fingers grappled—forever!—with the slick, tight knots at Amy's wrists and ankles. But when she finally came free I didn't talk at all. I just held her for what seemed like a long, long time.

"Katie?" Amy loosened her arms from around my neck and looked up at me, yellow light flickering across her face. "Promise you won't leave me again."

"Oh, Amy, I promise, honey, I promise."

Amy buried her face in my jacket and hugged me tight. "Tell me again how the police are going to rescue us," she said.

Were they? How? Would they take the dam apart and lower the lake so we could get out? Would Officer Dietz come swimming in like Aquaman? How would they know we were in here, anyway? The babysitter wouldn't know. She'd just know we weren't home. If someone had heard me screaming... But how would they know to look here?

"Katie? Tell me." Amy pulled away and tugged at my finger.

"Oh, Amy." I stroked her hair, holding her close. "Katie?"

"Let's go, Ames. We're getting out of here." If we hurried, we might make it out before water shut off the entrance. We had to.

I picked up the lantern. I closed my hand around Amy's. We started down. The cave flashed yellow and black, yellow and black, as if lit by a strobe light. Somewhere in the back of my mind it registered that the kerosene was almost gone, but I couldn't handle that at the moment; I flicked the thought away.

Then the yellow light spilled across the cave like liquid gold, and we were there, at the water. I moved the lantern in a semicircle, looking for the mouth of the cave.

Yellow and black. Yellow and black.

Where was it? Where had it been? Try to remember, try to find the place.

Yellow and black.

It had to be there.

But it wasn't.

I couldn't even remember where it had been.

"Katie?"

I sucked in a deep breath. "Yes, Ames."

"How are we gonna get out?"

"I don't know yet, honey. I'm thinking."

Deep inside me, though, I knew.

My mind ricocheted like a pinball, looking for another way out.

Water, rising imperceptibly, lapped against the edges of the cave.

All at once, I was flooded with the calm certainty of what I had to do.

"Amy, we're going back to the cavern."

"Why?"

"Tell you when we get there."

The long crawl back up to the cavern was bad enough, but what really hurt was telling Amy I was going to have to break my promise. When I told her I was leaving she screamed and clung to me. Even after I explained why and told her again and again that everything was going to be okay, she'd only be alone for a short time, I'd leave the light with her, I practically had to pry her off me, finger by finger. It felt like ripping off part of my body.

Down again, down to the water. I had to feel my way, it was so dark.

A cold wetness in my shoe told me when I'd reached water. I kept walking, and the cold crept up my legs. I stopped when it reached my knees. It was quiet, except for the soft swish of water when I moved. Amy wasn't crying anymore. When I turned around toward the passageway I could make out the dim yellow and black, yellow and black, but facing the way I had to go, it was just plain black.

Now. Do it.

I couldn't see the walls of the cave anymore, but, standing there, I had this strange sense of where they were. They were moving. They were squeezing in on me, making a tight little space where the air was so thin, no matter how hard you sucked in your breath you still couldn't get enough.

The rushing noise, like a tidal wave far away, grew inside my head, roared, broke and crashed over me, and the black water was rising.

I whirled around and ran out of the water, up the passageway again. A blue bolt of pain jagged up my leg and I collapsed on the ground, heaving for breath.

The walls of the passageway flickered yellow and black.

Amy began to cry.

Slowly, as if I were a puppet controlled by some force other than my own, I stood and walked into the pitch-black water. The cold crept up my legs, to my hips, my waist, my armpits. I took a deep breath and went under.

There was a ringing sound, like the sound of a rubber ball when it bounces on asphalt. My heart beat wildly in my ears. When I opened my eyes I saw black, so I shut them again and groped around with my hands.

Where was that opening?

My hands found the rough wall of the cave. They slid along it, searching, but I knew I was too high now, I'd been rising to the surface, I couldn't stay down. I came up for air, then really dove hard under, frogging with my legs to stay down.

Solid rock. I felt solid rock.

No good. I came up, took another breath. Then back down, walking along the wall with my hands.

It had to be here somewhere.

I scissored hard with my legs, reached way out and then there it was. A nothing. Kicking gently, I followed my arms through the nothing. I kept on through the nothing until my lungs burned.

I pulled up through the water into the air and drank in a glorious breath.

Chapter Seventeen

Bye, Kate!"

"Bye!" Standing on the curb outside school the following Wednesday, I leaned on a crutch and waved to a guy who'd never said word one to me before.

"Hey, Kate. Need a ride home?" A girl this time.

"No, thanks, I've got one."

Weird. Here I'd thought that when the whole story came out I'd be a permanent outcast. I'd had visions of kids in whispered huddles pointing at me. Or bombarding me with mystery meat in the cafeteria.

"See you tomorrow!" This from a couple of kids I'd never seen before.

"All right." Instead, everybody was treating me as if I were some kind of a hero. That's how the story in the newspaper turned out. Teenage Girl Saves Sister. It made me sound like Wonder Woman or something. The fact that I didn't actually haul Amy out of the cave—the divers did—didn't seem to matter. The fact that I'd taken those coins didn't, either. Maybe Wonder Woman-type stories sell newspapers, who knows?

But the money did matter to Officer Dietz and Officer Bradley. First, Officer Dietz told me that the coins belonged to my parents because they were found on our property, and no one else—including Dion—had a legal claim. So, unless Mom and Dad wanted to file charges, which they didn't, I hadn't technically committed a crime.

Then Officer Bradley lit into me. I had lucked out this time, he said, but he didn't want to see me embarking on a life of crime and all that. Plus the bit about withholding evidence and endangering my entire family. He really let me have it. Afterward I felt much better. Everyone else was being entirely too nice about the whole thing.

"Katharyn?"

It was Jessamyn. I hadn't seen her since Saturday morning. Her eyes met mine, then skittered away. "Katharyn, I—I didn't know Amy was in trouble. I really didn't."

"I know, Jessamyn."

"If I had I wouldn't have—I would have helped you find her." Jessamyn seemed close to tears.

"I know you would have."

Jessamyn looked down. She picked at the nubby things on her raw-silk blouse. "I'm glad you understand. Nick doesn't. He says I was cold and heartless to care more about skiing than about you and Amy. We're not going out for a while, I guess."

I didn't know what to say, so I didn't say anything. Then Jessamyn said: "Katharyn? Do you think you could talk to Nick? Tell him, you know, I do care about you guys and I would have helped if I'd known, and anyway he was there, too, and so he shouldn't really blame me because you don't?"

"I, uh, sure, I'll talk to him if you want."

Jessamyn flashed me one of her brilliant smiles. "Thanks." She glanced at the cast on my ankle. "You're not walking home, are you?"

"No, I've got a ride."

"Who wi... Oh." A station wagon cruised up to the curb. Kirk leapt out. Jessamyn opened her mouth to say something, then shut it. Kirk opened the door for me.

"Well," Jessamyn said. "See ya?"

"Sure. See ya." Jessamyn spun on her heel and walked away.

Kirk helped me into the car, tossed my crutches into the back seat, then sprinted to the driver's seat. "Hey, I figured something out," he said.

"What?"

Kirk eased the car into the street. "Well, remember what old Ida Mae said? About John Calais always playing mean tricks on Dion?"

"Um-hmm. You know, I kinda feel sorry for the guy. That picture of him we had, he looked like a real sad kid. It was like child abuse what they did to him. People like that get messed up, and it's not their fault."

"Thank you, Dr. Freud. You'd feel a lot less sorry for him if Ida Mae hadn't been spying out her window Saturday. It's a good thing she decided to call the cops after all, or the divers wouldn't have been there when you got out of the water. You'd have permanently screwed up your ankle getting to a phone. Not to mention Amy..."

"Don't even think it." On the windshield, raindrops formed. One bumped into another, gobbled it up, then slid to the bottom of the glass. I sighed. "I still feel kind of bad about that concussion I gave him."

"He'll recover. They have real good doctors in jail. Anyway, as I was saying before you changed the subject, there was hardly any money in that box. Not enough for an inheritance, even before you, uh..."

"It seemed like a lot to me," I mumbled.

"You worry too much about money."

"I know."

Kirk fiddled—longer than necessary, I thought—with the wiper knob. "The thing is," he said, "I bet that whole inheritance thing was just another mean trick. A test."

"How do you mean?"

"I called a wine expert yesterday. He said some 1928 Bordeaux are holding up real well. I asked him what 'real well' meant, and he said a thousand dollars."

"For one bottle of wine?"

"Yep."

"Wow." I thought about that. "There was a lot of wine in there. A hundred bottles, maybe."

"Yep. Probably not all of it was that valuable. But if even half of it was, Dion flunked the test. He smashed his inheritance."

Then there had been a real treasure. Worth thousands and thousands of dollars. It had been right under my nose; it had belonged to my family. And I had missed it. It was my fault it was gone.

Kirk pulled over in front of our house and shut off the motor. It was quiet except for the tinny sound of rain on the car roof.

The funny thing was, I didn't feel that bad about it. Oh, I felt bad for my parents—they could definitely have used the money—but I knew they wouldn't be super mad at me. Money wasn't that big a deal for them.

And somehow, treasure didn't seem all that important to me anymore, either.

Kirk turned to me. "Kate?"

"Yeah?"

"Did you ever—when you were in that cave, did your life pass in front of you?"

"Not really. At first I was so busy acting brave for Amy, I didn't have time to think about stuff like that." I paused. "I did think of some things I wished I'd done differently, though."

"Like what?"

"Well, it's like the stuff I was so worried about wasn't the really important stuff. Does that make any sense?"

Kirk looked at me and nodded. "Yeah," he said. "Yeah, it does." Then he got out of the car and came around to help me out. We walked toward the path in the rain.

"I did that when I heard about what happened," he said. "Wished I'd done something different. Something I'd been wanting to do, but . . ."

We were right under the kissing hedge now. Kirk stood close, his light, light eyes searching my face.

"What?" I whispered.

Kirk slid his arms around my waist and slowly pulled me to him. He brushed his lips against mine, pulled back, searched my face again. Then we were kissing, a long, lingering kiss. The earth wobbled beneath my one good foot, but Kirk's arms held me steady. We were still kissing when a bloodcurdling scream jerked us apart.

"Kaaaaatieeeee!" Amy pounded down the path, Cyrano puffing along at her heels. "Guess what!" she said.

"What?"

"Dad was fixing the ceiling, and guess what!"

"What?" Kirk asked, grinning at me.

"It bwoke. It fell down. It gonked him on the head and got white stuff all over." Amy was convulsed by a sudden giggle attack.

"Is Dad all right?"

"Hi, guys!" Dad poked his head out the front door, then walked down the path toward us. He looked like a powdered doughnut.

Amy put her hands on her hips and shouted, "Dad, you better fix this house. It's a weck! It's a disaser era!"

"Hush," I said.

* * * * *

COMING IN MARCH

DROPOUT BLUES

by Arlene Erlbach

"I'm quitting and that's final!"

"If you quit school, I don't want you living in my house anymore," my dad says. "Just see who's going to pay for your clothes, records and makeup then!"

"I'll pay for them," I tell him.

"Good. Find a job and see how easy it is."

"Fine. I will. You wait and see."

"Try it," he answers. "You think you have such great skills?"

"Why do you upset your father like that?" my mother asks.

"I'm not trying to upset him. He's upsetting me. I'm not asking *him* to leave home, am I?"

Now that Chris had made the big decision, what will be her next step?

DOB-1

QUANTITY	BOOK #	ISBN #	TITLE	AUTHOR	PRICE
☐	1	98001-9	Does Your Nose Get in the Way, Too?	Arlene Erlbach	$2.25
☐	2	98002-7	Lou Dunlop: Private Eye	Glen Ebisch	$2.25
☐	3	98003-5	Toughing it Out	Joan Oppenheimer	$2.25
☐	4	98004-0	Lou Dunlop: Cliffhanger	Glen Ebisch	$2.25
☐	5	98005-7	Guys, Dating and Other Disasters	Arlene Erlbach	$2.25
☐	6	98006-5	All Our Yesterdays	Stuart Buchan	$2.25
☐	7	98007-8	Sylvia Smith-Smith	Peter Nelson	$2.25
☐	8	98008-6	The Gifting	Ann Gabhart	$2.25
☐	9	98009-4	Bigger is Better	Sheila Schwartz	$2.25
☐	10	98010-8	The Eye of the Storm	Susan Dodson	$2.25
☐	11	98011-6	Shock Effect	Glen Ebisch	$2.25
☐	12	98012-4	Kaleidoscope	Candice Ransom	$2.25
☐	13	98013-2	A Kindred Spirit	Ann Gabhart	$2.25
☐	14	98014-0	The Right Moves	M. K. Kauffman	$2.25
☐	15	98015-9	Lighten Up, Jennifer	Kathlyn Lampi	$2.25
☐	16	98016-7	Red Rover, Red Rover	Joan Hess	$2.25
☐	17	98017-5	Even Pretty Girls Cry at Night	Merrill Joan Gerber	$2.25
☐	18	98018-3	Angel in the Snow	Glen Ebisch	$2.25
☐	19	98019-1	The Haunting Possibility	Susan Fletcher	$2.25
☐	20	98020-5	Dropout Blues	Arlene Erlbach	$2.25

Your Order Total $ _____

☐ (Minimum 2 Book Order)

Add Appropriate Sales Tax $ _____

Postage and Handling   .75

I Enclose   _____

Name _____

Address _____

City _____

State/Prov. _____ Zip/Postal Code _____

BOCR-2

SPACE SAVING RACK

...s on this handsome and sturdy book rack. The hand-rubbed walnut finish will blend into your library decor with quiet elegance, providing a practical organizer for your favorite hard-or soft-covered books.

Only $9.95

Approximately 16" x 8" when assembled

Assembles in seconds!

To order, rush your name, address and zip code, along with a check or money order for $10.70* ($9.95 plus 75¢ postage and handling) payable to *Crosswinds*.

Crosswinds
Book Rack Offer
901 Fuhrmann Blvd.
P.O. Box 1396
Buffalo, NY 14269-1396

Offer not available in Canada.

*New York and Iowa residents add appropriate sales tax.